Lydia's Dream

Also by the same author:

To Travel Hopefully:
22 Years in the RAF Medical Branch

Reuben the Fisherman:
A tale of Roman occupied Palestine

LYDIA'S DREAM

LYDIA ,THE ROMAN WOMAN WHO SAW
HISTORY MADE

DON SNUGGS

Matador
9 Priory Business Park
Kibworth Beauchamp
Leicestershire LE8 0RX, UK
Tel: (+44) 116 279 2299
Fax: (+44) 116 279 2277
Email: books@troubador.co.uk
Web: www.troubador.co.uk/matador

ISBN 978-1783062-881

British Library Cataloguing in Publication Data.
A catalogue record for this book is available from the British Library.

Typeset in Book Antiqua by Troubador Publishing Ltd
Printed and bound in the UK by TJ International, Padstow, Cornwall

Matador is an imprint of Troubador Publishing Ltd

For Sandie

AUTHOR'S NOTES

Little is known about Pontius Pilate and his wife. Pilate's origins are lost in the mists of time; various authorities have named his place of birth as Germany, and others as Italian Gaul, but irrespective of this he has gained a place in history. Remembered by some as a tyrant, others a pragmatic ruler, and others a misunderstood man, his claim to fame remains that he allowed a Jewish preacher, Jesus of Nazareth, to be executed, although he had declared him innocent of any crime.

As a ruler of Roman-occupied Judea, a province of Palestine – for some ten years, his tasks were, firstly, to keep the peace by force of arms if necessary, to collect the taxes for Tiberius the emperor, and to supervise the main public works required in a functional Roman country at that time, such as roads, water supplies and maintenance of public buildings – the infrastructure of the state.

So far as the indigenous natives of the subjugated country were concerned, he had little to do with their politics unless they impinged on, or threatened, the Pax Romana. So far as we can tell by what has been written about his affairs, he had a total contempt for the religion of the Jews, though religion and politics in Palestine were virtually the same thing. Being a normal Roman citizen himself, he was a religious person, as were all Romans, but worshipped many strange gods and would today be referred to as a pagan.

But he was an officer of senior rank, representative of

the emperor. He was requested by the Sanhedrin, the Jewish legislature which functioned from the Temple, to execute a prisoner they had found guilty of death according to their legal code. The prisoner was charged with claiming that he was the King of the Jews and the Sanhedrin used this spurious claim as evidence of high treason against Tiberius, and ordered that he should therefore be put to death as a rebel. But the Romans had the prerogative of executing prisoners, having removed this facility from the Jews when they overran the country in BC 63.

But Pilate, having examined the prisoner, found him to be innocent of any crime, and according to some sources, if he would not help them to get rid of this man, as the Jews demanded, they had to assume that he, Pilate, was not a worthy servant and representative of the emperor. With this pressure upon him, he agreed to provide the execution party and the prisoner was promptly dispatched. But Pilate annoyed the Sanhedrin by putting a written notice on the gibbet declaring that this prisoner was in fact the King of the Jews, and refused to remove it until the prisoner had expired.

Pilate was not a fan of the Jews and further upset them later by desecrating their Temple worship area with pagan artefacts. As a result, he was told by Emperor Tiberius to be more diplomatic and not to endanger the peace. He was recalled to Rome for some unknown reason soon after this episode, and walks out of history, some myths saying he was murdered and others that he committed suicide. It was not until 1961, however, that evidence was found by archaeologists in Israel confirming that he had actually ever existed!

His wife, however, gets little mention. All we know is that she had a bad dream about this prisoner the night before he was executed, and was convinced that he was innocent. So vivid was her dream that she begged her husband to let him go, or at least to have nothing to do with the whole affair – but Pilate chose to ignore this advice, and the rest is history.

This is the only reference to her in the New Testament. We do not know her name or origins, so in my imagination have given her both. Her family tree also gives some indication of her subsequent life and behaviour. There was a medieval myth that eventually she became a Christian convert, but the people of medieval times often formulated stories about biblical people, with little or no evidence to support them, and usually for their own ends.

I have built a life for her as a Roman aristocrat. As with all Roman women, she was allowed to own and run a business, and to have property and inheritance rights, but was not allowed to vote or be a member of the legislature. Even so, many women had much influence through male relatives who held important positions within the Roman state.

But, like her husband, she has obtained notoriety which has lasted for two thousand years, although she is remembered only when the Easter story is told. Pilate's name is remembered every time the creed is spoken in the Christian Church, but her role in history is mentioned only once a year when the Easter story is recounted.

However, these two little known people, who we now know did exist, have made a greater impact on society than any husband and wife had ever made before their time or have since, and without them western civilisation would not have developed as it did.

CHAPTER 1

It was a bright spring morning, but something was wrong, very wrong. The day was heading for disaster – Lydia felt it in her bones!

The poor cat had just given birth to five kittens, all dead, and now the animal lay in a stupor on the floor of the atrium, mewing piteously as its life ebbed away in a pool of blood. The peacocks in the garden, normally the most vocal of creatures, were silent for some reason this morning. Unusually a flight of birds were flying high toward the east in a strange formation which in itself was ominous. What did it all mean?

A storm threatened; she could hear the rumble of thunder over the Judean hills to the west and could see the continuous flicker of lightning in the distance. The city was restless and the noise of the crowd percolated through to the palace gardens. There were shouts of protest and anger – some violent demonstration was going on. Oh, she was sick of this country and its people and yearned to return to the civilized life of their villa in Rome. They had their own slaves to look after them in Rome who were all well known to them and friendly. The slaves here, however, were a sullen, uncooperative lot, reluctant to do anything more than their duties, irrespective of the punishments handed out to them by her majordomo when they misbehaved.

The air for the time of year had been unusually hot

and humid over the last two days. She'd slept badly the night before and had had a particularly vivid dream which continued to haunt her. A man had been hauled up above her with tied hands and feet, and he'd looked down on her and smiled with a look of pity on his thin face. She heard him say, "This all will pass, Lydia, but I won't," as he looked around at her palatial surroundings. Oh, that voice! It was still there as the dream faded, but she could hear it still, impressed upon her memory. What did it mean?

She jerked out of her reverie and looked at the garden, where the spring sunshine now shone dully on the newly flowering plants. The bright flowers would have appeared beautiful to her any other day, but today they just looked garish.

She started suddenly as her husband, the procurator, called from the house, "Lydia, are you there? I've got to go out. There's a delegation from the Temple who wish to see me urgently at court," and off he went in a clatter of spurs and body armour.

Why did he always have to wear that noisy gear? she thought irritably, even though she knew it would not be the first time someone had tried to knife him in the back.

Oh, these people. She was worried about her husband and his safety, she was also aware that he was not the flavour of the month with the emperor either. He was too outspoken and when annoyed with the country put up taxes for the locals to teach them a lesson. It might keep him in with Rome, but it made the locals more unpleasant to him and he had to keep a firm grip on them at all times. She knew what he was like, and how far he could go, but one day he'd go too far and that would be that. He'll upset either the gods or the locals or Caesar, and she would then be a widow – and if it was Rome he upset, there would be no widow's pension, and then how would she survive?

So it was a bad morning of misgivings. To take her mind off her woes, she told her personal maid, Miriam, to come and sing to her accompanied by the lute. Miriam had a nice voice, but she had her moods and did not always please her mistress, and was unable to do so today.

Later that morning her husband returned, looking annoyed, hot and sweaty.

"What did the delegation want?" she asked him.

"Oh, they've got some agitator who was preaching against them. I was forced to listen to their rant. I called him in but couldn't find anything wrong with him and said so. He was another one who claimed to be a messiah, one of many – they seem to spring up all over the place. He'll soon be forgotten, but this one has really got up the noses of the Temple lot!"

"Who was this one, then?" she asked.

"Oh, some young chap from Nazareth. He seemed harmless to me, but they accused him of blasphemy and they want him out of the way – probably hit a raw nerve by exposing what they've been doing. Anyway, I'm not going to get involved in their theological nonsense and argue with those bigots!"

Lydia felt something grip her gut. "Was he a man with a thin face, black hair, blue eyes and a mole on his chin?" she asked.

The procurator looked at her with raised eyebrows. "Yes, he was. Why, do you know him?"

Lydia fell at her husband's feet and gripped his legs, "Don't have anything to do with him," she pleaded in absolute terror. "I saw him in my dream last night. He spoke to me; he's innocent and if you hurt him it will mean disaster for all of us!"

Pilate laughed, "Rubbish , he's only a peasant. I've told them to deal with it; they want to execute him for blasphemy. For all I care they can do so – I've washed my hands of the case. Now then, is my meal ready? Then I must have a lie down, this heat is getting to me."

The storm broke during the afternoon; it was a violent storm with terrifying thunder and lightning, a howling gale of wind but strangely little rain, and the sky was as black as night for a time. It was the worst storm in living memory, it was claimed by those who watched the weather. However, the procurator slept fitfully through it all on his couch until evening, when he was awakened by his secretary.

"Now what?" he exclaimed, "Can't I get any peace?"

"Sorry, sir," said the man, "but there's a delegation from the Temple again to see you. They say its urgent – same lot as this morning."

"What do they want now, for heaven's sake?" asked Pilate, now thoroughly irritated at the thought of another session with these people, he couldn't abide their sycophancy and the veiled threats they always used if they couldn't get their own way.

"Oh alright, I'll see them in the hall. Show them in."

He got up, put on his armoured vest and uniform hat, and went down the steps into the hall.

They were all standing there, about twenty of them, looking very solemn. *Like a lot of sheep,* he thought, *but not as useful!*

"Well," he demanded "What now?"

Their spokesman started, "Sir, we know that in your wisdom you gave us permission..."

Pilate broke in, "Oh stop the charm, it doesn't become you. What do you want?" he shouted. "Spit it out!"

"Well, sir, the man you condemned to death this morning..." began the spokesman.

"No, you did." broke in Pilate. "Nothing to do with me. I washed my hands of it all and you saw me," he said scornfully.

"Ah, but your men executed him," said the spokesman craftily.

" Get on with it then!" shouted Pilate.

"Of course, excellency," replied the spokesman obsequiously, "but the criminal said he would come back to life in three days. Can you authorize a guard on the body? There are some very violent ones among his followers, one cut off the ear of the servant of the High Priest – which I'm sure you know as you seem to know everything else, sir – and if they did steal the body and tell everyone he was still alive, it wouldn't do your reputation a lot of good. After all, as I said , your men crucified him, did they not? The consequences would be disastrous for us all, and we are certain that the emperor, if he got to hear of it,would be most displeased."

"Alright," Pilate said testily. "I'll do that, now go away and trouble me no more. You've got what you wanted and also got a known terrorist released. Barabas of all people! Now we've got to deal with that villain. Get out before I change my mind." And with that Pilate turned to go. The delegation backed out of the palace and slunk off into the night. Pilate noticed that two elderly men were still there. "What do you want?" he demanded rudely.

"Sir," said one, "I am Joseph of Aramithea, and Nicodemus here I believe you know."

Pilate replied, "Oh yes, he spoke to my wife at the last palace reception for the High Priest."

Pilate looked closely at them and his voice softened, "Of course, I remember, you're both lawyers – of the better sort." He laughed, "If there is such a thing! What can I help you with?"

"Could we have the body?" asked Nicodemus. "He was a good man – not one of the delegation are fit to have tied his shoelaces. Joseph here would like to bury him in his own prepared tomb in his garden."

Pilate looked at these two decent old men and felt – strangely, for he had been brought up as a Roman soldier – a surge of pity. "Yes of course," he said softly. "You do just that and I'll get my secretary to give you a chit authorising removal of the body and the burial. Good night to you both."

He turned and walked away to have his meal. On the way to the dining room he called into his secretary's office and told him the gist of the conversation he'd had with the men. He told him to make a record of it all and write out the chit for the two lawyers. He also instructed him to get the palace guard commander to arrange for the tomb to be secured for the next three days and nights, and having had a busy day went off duty with instructions that he was not to be disturbed unless the end of the world came!

The officer commanding security and in charge of the palace guard was surprised to be summoned so late in the day to the secretary's office. He'd had a long and tiring day controlling the demonstration on the streets, which had culminated in the execution of three criminals. It was always a tense time on these occasions; they attracted troublemakers like flies to a honey pot, and a lot of them had to be arrested and put in the pound, to be released later when all was quiet.

Crowds always gathered to see such spectacles. The general public seemed to have a huge appetite for watching calculated cruelty and he was often appalled at their thirst for blood – they were probably glad it wasn't them being flogged through the streets, having not been caught themselves! Having served in many theatres as a soldier, he was used to the discipline of the service, and the indiscipline of the crowd offended his sense of order, without which a population or indeed a country could not flourish. He knew this behaviour was not confined to Palestine, but it was no easier to deal with wherever you served – Gaul, Spain or Egypt, and they really were savages there!

He'd needed a lot of patience today with this lot. Funny, he mused, riots the world over are not just a group of troublemakers but a solid mass of humanity behaving as though chained to each other – anything for a punch up, and why not burn a few shops while they're at it? Anything is fair game!

This one today, however, was a bit different. There had been a lot of women wailing, which had been quite eerie, and enough to put you off your stroke. They'd wept uncontrollably, though hadn't tried to stop the procession to the gallows – but their wailing! He'd not forget that for a long time.

So, as he mounted the stairs to the secretary's office, he was tired. *What's the boss want now?* he thought. He knocked on the door and entered when the secretary's called.

The secretary was at his desk; he was a staff officer and wore the purple-lined tunic of his rank of tribune. He outranked the commanding officer, who was a centurion, but they were on familiar terms, both having seen service and having achieved promotion to their rank by virtue of their abilities in the army. They had great respect for each other too, having both served with distinction in many parts of the empire.

"Ah, Claudius," said the tribune, "do come in and take the weight off your feet. I didn't realise it would be you on duty. Haven't seen you for a bit, been on leave?" he asked, smiling.

"I have indeed, sir," he replied, "and not glad to be back with that lot we had to deal with today."

The tribune laughed, "No, it's been quite a day."

"Right, sir, what do you want me for?" asked Claudius.

"Now then, two men have come for permission to take the body of one of the three executed today. The Temple don't like bodies hanging on the gibbet over their Sabbath, you know, and the boss has agreed that two of the late lamented's friends can have his body and bury it their own tomb – they'll be up in a minute to collect the chit to take to your chaps at the site. Then, because the Jews are a superstitious lot and think that he might be stolen by his other followers and used for political purposes, they want the tomb sealed for at least three days and you are to arrange a detail to do this. It will have to be supervised as this is high politics and rather sensitive, so see what you can do. Don't make a lot of fuss about it and attract an audience; be as low key as you can. Incidentally, the Temple lot think he said he will come back to life in three days, would you believe it – pigs might fly! But if his followers did steal the body, it would soon bring down the administration. Got that? Give the two men their chit; they're down in the hall and will tell you how to find the tomb."

The secretary looked out of the window. "Be glad when today's over," he grunted. "I'm now off to bed. I'll leave you to it."

The commanding officer went downstairs, got the details from Joseph, handed him the chit and went to find his orderly officer.

The orderly officer had gone to bed early, having had a busy day at the execution, but Claudius woke him up and gave him his orders.

"But all my men are exhausted, sir," the orderly officer said. "There are a couple of troopers in the cells though who both went AWOL after the crucifixion today, and when we found them they were roaring drunk." His face brightened. "Yes, I'll use them. That's a good punishment, and will teach them a lesson."

The two malcontents were brought out of the cells, given their duties and marched off with a non-commissioned officer leading them to the tomb. There, with the help of Joseph and Nicodemus, they covered the entrance to the tomb with a large slab of quarried stone and placed the emperor's seal on it – removal of which, by unauthorised persons, would automatically attract the death penalty.

The officer, then ascertaining that the men were aware of their duties and had enough food for the night until relieved in the morning, left them, telling them that the orderly officer and his staff would come sometime in the night to check that all was well.

The two troopers settled down for the night, played a game of cards and had a good grumble about discipline, but as the night wore on the effects of the alcohol caught up with them and they dozed off. When the orderly officer arrived, already in a bad mood at being awoken for such an onerous duty, and found them asleep, he immediately kicked them awake and said that as he had caught them asleep on duty, their punishment was either a flogging or to stay on guard for the full three nights. They chose the three nights of duty!

So, by the time the next day had passed and it was evening again, both guards were thoroughly exhausted, and irrespective of the threat of fatal consequences, gave into their tired bodies and fell sound asleep.

At first light, there was a tremendous crash as the huge stone covering the entrance to the tomb fell flat on the ground in a cloud of dust. Both men now were wide awake and let out a shout. They knew now what would happen to them – the seal in Caesar's name had been broken, which meant death – but were stunned by the noise. It was difficult for them to see exactly what was happening in the thick early morning mist, but one of the two peered into the tomb and it appeared to be empty! Being well aware that their dereliction of duty would mean they would be lucky to be alive this time tomorrow, or hanging on a wooden cross in agony fighting to breathe until death mercifully released them, they decided that discretion was the better part of valour and quickly decided to run – but to where? They were in a garden with a high fence around it and the orderly officer was due to make his rounds. In blind panic they scrambled up the rock face in which the tomb was cut and into the bushes above. As they paused for breath, they looked down and saw a young woman wearing a grey cloak with her head covered approach the tomb. She also carried a bag from which it looked like bunches of herbs protruded. When she reached the tomb and saw the stone cover removed they heard her say, "What have you done with him?" She fell onto the ground and lay prostrate with grief.

As they watched, the tall figure of a man appeared out of the mist. She must have sensed his presence because she looked up and cried, "Where is he? You must know, you work here in the garden?"

One of the two hiding guards whispered to the other, "Who's that? I recognise his face from somewhere."

"Shush," said the other, "they'll hear us."

Suddenly they saw the tall figure look down at the woman and say something, at which the woman leapt to her feet and let out a shout of sheer delight. As she moved toward him, the figure vanished along with the woman into the mist.

"Come on," said one of the guards. "Let's get out of here – there's something funny going on."

At that moment the orderly officer and his escort arrived, quickly summed up the situation and ordered his men to cover the area. They discovered the two fugitives hiding in the bushes and handcuffed them.

"Right, you scum," he snarled, "now you will die. Come on, back to the barracks, nothing we can do here, I'd better let the householder know what's happened."

Suddenly more locals arrived and were running up the hill, but the Romans were more concerned with getting their prisoner back to the guardroom than with anything else.

Back at the barracks, both men were put in the dungeon to await the arrival of their executioner, but after a few minutes there was a commotion outside the door and one of the Jewish elders from the Temple Authorities pushed his way into the cell.

"What happened?" he demanded harshly "Who took the body?"

"We don't know, sir," they both replied.

"There must have been an earthquake," said one hopefully.

"Listen, and listen carefully," said the elder. "The followers of this man attacked you and stole his body, didn't they?"

"No," said the guard, "we saw nothing like that."

"You did if I say so, and I'll make it worth your while and get you out of here if that is what you'll say. You've got to make the choice: either agree with me or you will be hanged before night. Got that? If you choose right, you will both be rich men, as will your orderly officer. Come on; let's have a bit of common sense, shall we?"

Later that day, the procurator was working in his office when his secretary came into speak with him. He looked troubled.

"Sir," he began, "did you hear what happened last night at the tomb you sealed?"

"No, I've not seen the night report yet, I'm waiting for Centurion Claudius to bring it in. Why, what happened?"

"The orderly officer got there just after the followers of the man had attacked the guards, broken open the tomb and stolen the body. The Jews want blood, yours preferably, sir. One of them apparently said that you had probably organised it yourself to discredit them."

Pilate looked at him in angry dismay. "Did they, by Jupiter! That's all we need. Now there will be real trouble; you'd better get the guard commander to double or even triple the patrols on the streets until it all blows over. And no, I do not, repeat not, want to see a delegation from the Temple. Tell them to sort out their own affairs or I will do it for them, and in the way they don't like – and then they'll really know about it. Tell them that, and by the gods I mean it. I'm fed up to the back teeth with the lot of them!"

He stood up, picked up the goblet of wine he always had when working at his desk and stamped out into the atrium. "Lydia," he shouted, "bring me some more wine, and a lot of it."

Lydia came into the room with another flask of his favourite wine. "What's wrong?" she asked, looking at her husband's flushed and angry face. He told her.

"I told you nothing good would come of it if you dealt with that man," she said. "Now we've got to live with it." She thought for a moment. "You know, those Jewish leaders at the Temple would say anything and blame anyone to get their own way. I have a feeling they are upset because he probably did rise from the dead. After all, they wouldn't make a fuss about nothing, would they?"

So he's still here then, she thought, *but I wonder how much longer we will be after this!*

CHAPTER 2

After a few days the fuss did die down, but it was now time for the procurator and his staff to return to Tiberius – his main residence in the province – following his annual visit to the capital. He was still angry and annoyed at the events of the past week, but as he prepared to move out, Lydia said she was glad to leave and did not wish to visit the capital again.

She was still thoughtful and upset by what had happened to her husband, knowing that the Temple would make as much of it as they could, and she was still haunted by the dream she'd had. Every time she was not thinking of day-to-day affairs, she could hear the voice; it intruded on her thoughts continually, and she still grieved for her beloved cat who had died so cruelly on that memorable day.

She had made tentative enquiries amongst her staff about the events of that week, but trying to start a conversation with staff members about the criminal who had been executed was difficult. She found they were reluctant to call him a criminal even though the law said he was and they were tight-lipped about it, suggesting this was just another example of Roman cruelty. Even her personal maid, Miriam, would not comment, only saying quietly, "Well, we'll see what the future holds, my lady."

So Lydia put on a brave face in front of the servants, but underneath she was terrified of the future for both herself and her husband – if only that voice would leave her alone! Then the final blow came: her husband was commanded to return to Rome on orders from the emperor as soon as possible. Tiberius was aging and was putting his house in order before he died. The Jewish authorities had complained in the past of Pilate's harshness, and word was that Pilate would be replaced by another procurator more sensitive to local opinion – the name Marcellus had been mentioned.

However, they were both glad to get back to the palace in Tiberius for the time being. At least it was quieter than the capital, and from the palace walls there was a superb view of the lake which in itself was calming to the spirit. The lake provided a good supply of fresh fish for the palace kitchens, and Lydia was most partial to the perch caught by the locals. Being a Roman city, their servants were more helpful than the Jewish servants in Jerusalem.

But if Pilate was to return to Rome at the earliest possible time, it would prove difficult to find transport of a style commensurate with Pilate's status, and local galleys were quite unsuitable. A suitable ship had to have room on board for not only the procurator and his family, but for all his household goods, his personal staff, horses and all the ceremonial gear needed for a person of his rank – that is, an appointee of the emperor. So he would, in all probability, have to wait for his successor to arrive so he could return on the same vessel: an ocean-going galley commensurate with his rank.

So, it was a period of waiting. Although surrounded by congenial staff in familiar surroundings, Lydia still wanted to get it over with and return to Rome, to the luxurious life at court with all her friends and family. She hoped that then her husband would be able to clear his name and continue with his career – if not in the court circles, at least in the army, where he was a very senior staff officer. She felt in her heart that any charges against him would be unjust. Yes he was a hard man but he was fair, and as procurator he had made enemies, but who did not in such high society? But that voice was still there, though she'd hoped she'd left it behind in the capital. What was she going to do? She prayed for deliverance from it to her household gods, but they just stared blankly back, as uncommunicative as the stone they were made of!

The guard commander was summoned to the secretary's office the day after the news of the recall. Centurion Florus was the most senior officer after the secretary, who was a staff officer. Florus was responsible for all the ceremonial duties, and his cohort of some hundred men guarded the palace and the life of the procurator. As such he had his fingers in many pies and also ran an efficient intelligence service in the province.

"We've got to arrange the shipping of the boss and all his belongings, Centurion Florus," said the secretary. "There are a lot of items, personnel and animals to go, so you'll have to draw up an inventory of it all and then get someone down to Caesarea to see the movement officer at the port. You'll have to arrange transport there with an escort, arrange accommodation overnight prior to boarding, and then arrange the return of transport back here with the new procurator. First you'll have to liase with lady Lydia to do the inventory, though I suggest you initially do this yourself. You can use one of my clerks to write it all down and don't forget to keep one copy for me, one for movements and one for the file. Have you got that? Oh, and you better send a reliable chap down to the port to get it all underway. Who are you going to send? Have you thought of that? Perhaps your number two; he was garrison commander at Caesarea before he came here I believe, so should know his way around."

The centurion had been busy taking notes as the secretary talked to him. He looked up eventually, saying, "Right, sir, we'll get started. Any idea when the ship is due?"

"Yes, we've got about a month so you'll need to get going quickly," said the secretary. "Be as efficient as you can – the boss is not in the best of moods and has bitten a few heads off already, mine included." He laughed ruefully. "But that's the way he is."

The centurion also laughed. "Have to hope his successor is more even-tempered then, but if you will allow me, sir, I'd like young Centurion Augustus to do this. It would be a good training exercise for him; he's a very level-headed chap and could do with the experience, having only recently done his senior officer management course."

"Alright, Florus, but you supervise him. I don't want anything to go wrong," replied the secretary.

The guard commander saluted his superior officer and went out to start proceedings.

Centurion Augustus was called in and informed of his duties. He was pleased to be given the task, not only because it got him away from the ceremonial duties and spit and polish, but it also meant he would be going back to see his friends. He liked Caesarea and had got on well with the locals when he was in charge of the port garrison. He had also contributed to the building of the local synagogue for the Jewish community, believing that good community relations by the occupying forces was good politics. So he was well known and respected and this was quite a nice little detail for him.

After making an appointment to see lady Lydia, he met her the following afternoon. He had never met her before and was rather concerned at how tired she looked. She was also rather vague and spoke as if she had something on her mind, but she seemed to be a pleasant person and was relatively easy to get on with. She was in fact very helpful, knowing the huge task Augustus had been given to do, and she was happy to direct her servants to cooperate with him, so he found it relatively easy to make the inventory of the household goods and chattels. However, he would have to speak to the secretary, she remarked, when it came to the horses and their accoutrements.

She asked him about where they would stay in Caeserea and if he knew the area, and he told her of his association with the town.

"That will be nice for you to see your friends again, do you get there often?" she asked him.

"No, not often. I try, though, to get home as often as possible, duty permitted."

"And where is that? Local?" she asked.

"Yes, my lady," he replied. "We've got a villa up the lake at Capernium."

"Oh, that's lovely," she replied. "The lake is very beautiful at this time of the year with all the gardens in bloom."

"Thank you, my lady," he replied. "Yes, it's about two months since I was last home, I had special leave because my servant had had an accident and broke his back. He fell off the roof doing some repairs and my wife had nobody to look after them, so I went home to sort it out. I needn't have worried though because a well-known preacher and healer was in the area and I asked him to come and have a look at poor old Decimus, who was in bed paralysed. He was paralysed from the waist down and I thought he'd die – well I've never heard of anyone who survived with a broken back."

"So what happened?" she asked.

"It was very interesting; he had quite a crowd around him, you know, hangers -on and a few of his friends. This was the first time I'd met him, though I'd heard a lot about him, but there was something special about this man who spoke so gently. So I waited until the crowd thinned a little and went up to him. He looked at me, smiled and said, 'What can I do for you, Augustus?', which floored me. He knew my name and Jews don't usually talk or even look at Romans if they can help it! I asked him if he would heal my servant who'd broken his back in a fall. I apologised for asking, and told him that, as a centurion, I didn't usually ask anyone to do anything for me, so would he help?"

He smiled, put his hand on my arm and said, 'Don't worry, when you get home, you'll find him up and about as usual.' And you know what, my lady, he was!

"The preacher then turned to the crowd. 'Did you hear that?' he said. 'This officer is not a Jew but he believes me, why don't you lot?' Or words to that effect. I asked him how he knew my name and he said, 'God even knows when a sparrow falls to earth; you are worth many sparrows.' I had to work that one out! Then he went on his way with a smile and a wave of his hand."

Lydia was most interested in the story and asked, "What sort of a man was he?"

"Oh, I remember him well," he said. "Tall chap, blue eyes, black hair and a mole on his chin, you couldn't miss it." He cried suddenly with alarm, "Madame! What's the matter? Are you ill?"

The lady had sat down and her face had gone white. "Was his name Jesus?" she whispered.

"Yes it was," he replied. "I'd forgotten that; the locals and his followers called him Master. Why, do you know him?"

"Oh dear," muttered Lydia. "I knew of him, he's dead now, executed by his own people. My husband interrogated him when he was charged with some misdemeanour concerning Jewish law and could find nothing wrong. He'd apparently accused his Temple people of hypocrisy and they never forgave him."

Augustus sighed, "I'm sorry to hear that; the preacher went about doing so much good for people who needed it, people like my servant. He did nothing wrong I'm sure. He was a good man and much loved."

"I've no doubt about that. Fancy killing such a man," replied Lydia. "The gossip was that he had come back to life, and the Temple accused my husband of encouraging his followers to steal his body and say he was still alive. It has left me very troubled and I don't know what to think. I'd like to know what happened, in fact something tells me I've got to find out, but I don't know where to turn for help. I know he's still alive, which must sound silly, but this has really got to me. I even dream about it now."

Augustus looked at his superior's wife with pity. *Money position and power aren't everything,* he thought, as he turned to his task.

CHAPTER 3

Within the month, Centurion Augustus had returned from Caesarea with the details of the move to the port for the sea journey to Rome, which was to be within the next two weeks. Confirmation had arrived by fast overland courier that Pilate's replacement would be, as was thought likely, Marcellus, and Pilate would be taken to Rome, where it was hoped he would arrive, wind and weather permitting, in about three weeks following embarkation on the same galley.

Lydia was relieved at the news of the proposed arrival of Marcellus, and hoped that the handover would go smoothly so there were no delays in starting for Rome.

Centurion Florus had done his homework, and her husband, even though he was still a bit upset at his summons home, remarked that Florus had done a good job. He pointed out to her that that was what he was paid for, but that Florus had gone the extra mile, and that was the important thing and made the difference between a good centurion and a very good one. He said he would put him in for a commendation when they got back. This pleased Lydia, as she knew how much work the officer had done to make the journey as comfortable as possible.

Lydia would be pleased to get started; busy she might be, but she was impatient to be off. They had been in Tiberius some eight years, so there were a lot of loose ends to tie up and a lot of good friends to say goodbye to. The move was indeed tinged with sadness. Tiberius was a lovely location to live, and she would miss the peace and quiet of the lake. However, when she went to bed each night she was exhausted because that voice continued to haunt her – the same words, 'this will all pass, but I wont' – and she needed a draught of wine to get her off to sleep, after which she would awake each morning with a thick head.

She'd never again mentioned the voice to her husband; she felt that he had enough to worry about, so bottled it up inside until she felt she would burst. When they had a few moments together he asked what was on her mind – he knew how much she wanted to get away, but also sensed her sadness at leaving.

Lydia was well aware that when they did get back to Rome her husband's future was uncertain, but that her father, the head of their depleted family, would be there to greet them. She could, if she remembered correctly, open her heart to him as he was a thoughtful man. She had lost her mother just after they arrived in Judea, and her older brother had been killed in battle somewhere in Asia when he was only twenty years old – gallantly, they were told, fighting dissident tribesmen. So apart from her father's sister, if she was still alive, Lydia was his sole blood relative.

Her father and she had corresponded over the years, and his letters were always comforting and full of happy thoughts. He was a very religious man who worshipped the gods and had read widely all the philosophers, ancient and modern. She assumed this was why he was a great philanthropist and would help anyone in distress, in body or mind. He had often expressed his frustration as a senator with those leaders of the State who desired to maintain the status quo to avoid any discomfort to their comfortable lives, without thinking of those less fortunate than themselves – thus earning for himself a certain amount of obloquy, and not a few enemies, when speaking in the senate.

However, as a very rich man with estates and many members of staff to manage them, she recalled that he was a good employer. When his wife died, he had said in a letter to Lydia that he realised his life had been blessed by the gods because he could have lost more than her. It could all have been worse because his daughter had married a reputed despot, but he was grateful that he, Gratus Lydias, had retained his good name, and nobody who really mattered thought badly of him, nobody that is except for Lydia's Aunt Aurelia, who lived in the seaside town of Herculaneum – if she was still alive.

Lydia had heard nothing from her for at least a year, and her father had not mentioned her in his letters. She was a strange old lady – she had appeared ancient to Lydia even before she left for Judea – who felt she was not quite of this world. She studied astrology to the point that it was all she ever wrote about, and Lydia usually failed to understand what she meant. She would not, she thought, be much of a companion.

The new procurator arrived and settled into the palace, spending two days with her husband while he handed things over. When all the ceremonies and administration details were completed, all was ready for their journey to Caesarea. The excellent Augustus had arranged transport and all the other particulars regarding security.

There were a lot of goods to go – having been in the post for so many years, they had collected a mass of personal items, some quite valuable, including many gifts given to them on their departure by the local dignitaries and their friends. The cavalry escort was ready, so early one morning, to miss the heat of the day, followed by a group of noisy pye-dogs, they set off on the one-hundred mile journey to the port of Caesarea. They stopped en route three times at government rest houses and eventually arrived at the port, where they were met by an honour guard and band, escorted by the garrison commander and the movement officer, who fussed around as all movement officers do. They then embarked on the ocean-going galley which was to take them to Rome and their future – *whatever that will be,* thought Lydia with a feeling of great disquiet. Hopefully, if the wind held fair, they should arrive within three weeks – it was good sailing weather the ship's captain said – and after goodbyes had been said, and the last trumpet note died away from the band, the galley cast off from the quay and they were on their way.

Lydia liked sailing, as a child her father had had a small sailing boat which they used on holiday, and being an accomplished swimmer she had no fear of the water. For the first time in weeks, she was able to relax and watch the world go by with few responsibilities, and she had not heard the disturbing voice telling her of his presence again.

The captain of the vessel was well aware of his prestigious passengers and his valuable cargo, and did all he could to make their voyage as comfortable as possible. He even arranged for Lydia and her husband to go ashore when they called in for water at two port stops on the way, so they could stretch their legs. He provided them with an armed guard, necessary in these troubled times, for he was totally responsible for his passengers, whoever they were as he explained to Pilate.

And three weeks to the day, they arrived at Ostia, the main sea port for Rome. As they docked, the movements officer, accompanied by a senior tribune, came aboard and with little ceremony took Pilate into the cabin. Lydia became worried as she waited for the men to come out, and was alarmed to hear raised voices. A few minutes later Pilate emerged looking very angry and told Lydia that he was under arrest on orders from the emperor, and that she was to go to her father's villa. Transport was arranged, and he would hopefully be in touch as soon as possible. She was given no further details, and after a terse farewell he stalked off the ship with his escort to where a troop of cavalry and two horses – one for Pilate and the other for the tribune – awaited for the journey to the fortress.

Lydia was overcome with a feeling of utter helplessness. How wonderful it had been to see Italy again and to know that only just a short distance away was their own home, and now in one fell swoop all had gone and she knew in her heart that she would never see her husband again. Apart from her father she had no one to turn to; arrested men had no friends, neither did their families. Never having had children – always a bone of contention between her and Pilate – she was on her own. Lydia did not know if her father was still alive; when she had last heard from him three months before, he had said that life was becoming a burden to him. So now her fear for the future had been confirmed – there appeared to be no future! She said in despair to her personal maid, "What am I going to do?"

A closed carriage awaited Lydia and her maid on the quayside, where two donkeys were in harness to pull the vehicle. They were to be escorted by four armed guards from the prison service, uncommunicative, surly, big men who, impatient to get her to her destination, and drove the outfit too quickly with little or no regard for the occupants. There was little respect for the wife of an arrested man, whatever his rank, and they wanted to get back to the tavern!

Lydia was too distressed to talk much and wept silently into her handkerchief. Her maid quietly told her, "Don't worry, my lady, I'm sure it's all a mistake and it will turn out alright."

"If only it were so," replied Lydia tremulously. "Not when the emperor sends for you I'm afraid." She was convinced she would never see her husband again, and remained silent for the rest of the two-hour journey.

He father's estate, one of six he possessed, was to the west of Rome. The main house was built on a hill with a view of the distant sea, and as they bounced along, she could hear to the east the sound of Rome – a dull, raucous roar which seemed to go on night and day. If she remembered aright, it sounded the same as the Jerusalem that they had left some three months ago. *All cities sound the same,* she thought; *everlasting turmoil, no place to live and remain sane!* But she had never thought when they left Jerusalem she would return like this, treated as a criminal's wife. Now, as far as society was concerned, she was a woman under the care of nobody. She didn't expect her father to reject her when he was told of the circumstances, but as a senator, he had to be aware of his privileged position, and could not afford to have it compromised by relatives accused of some criminal activity.

The carriage turned sharply into the drive of her father's villa. Throwing Lydia and her maid to one side, it rattled up the drive lined with cypress trees – she remembered them being planted all those years ago and now they were tall, mature trees – before coming to a grinding halt in front of the portico of the house. The house guard and his dog were there, as well as two men she did not know. As she extricated herself from the tumbled personal possessions in a muddle in the carriage, she took a deep breath, composed her face – a Roman matron never shows her feelings to strangers! – and alighted, to be greeted by an elderly grey-haired man.

"I'm Cassius, my lady," he said, bowing to her, "your father's majordomo. I trust you are well and had a good journey?"

"As well as could be expected," she replied. "The journey was most uncomfortable."

She turned at the sound of her maid shouting at the guards, who were unceremoniously throwing her possessions out of the carriage on to the paved area before the house. Before she could say anything the carriage and its reluctant escort were galloping down the drive in a cloud of dust.

"How is my father?" she asked.

"Will you come in, my lady, and sit down? There is

much to tell you," he replied, not meeting her enquiry with his eyes.

She followed him into the atrium; her maid was behind her, having gathered up her scattered belongings. It was just as she remembered it with the fountain and vases of flowers which gave such a lovely scent to the room. However, the chair her father always used was empty today. "Where is my father?" she said, peremptorily.

"I'm afraid, my lady, your father passed away two weeks ago. He was excited at your homecoming, but had been in poor health for the last year. He had a fall and two days later he died, I'm sorry to have to tell you. You have, my lady, my deepest sympathy. He tried to keep going, but the fall was just too much for him. He was a good man much loved by us all and is sorely missed."

Lydia sat down suddenly. *Poor father,* she thought, *he had a lonely life without any of us around, and now I take over that life.*

"Are you alright?" asked Cassius. "I'll get you a drink, my lady," and as he clapped his hands a servant girl brought Lydia a goblet of wine, curtsied and handed it to her.

"Thank you for telling me," she said as she took the drink from the girl. "Who is the other man who met me?"

"That is your father's lawyer, yours now if you wish to deal with him, but your father had great faith in him and I am sure he will be of great help to you. There is much for him to discuss with you, but now is not the time for that, and if I may be so bold, would ask you to follow the housemaid to your quarters upstairs. We can discuss all this when you have rested. You look worn out, my lady."

"Yes, I am, but before that, where is my father's body?" she asked, trying to restrain the tears.

"He did not wish to be cremated, my lady," he replied, "so we buried him just above the knoll at the back of the house – next to your mother's grave as he requested. And there is a letter he wrote to you when he knew he was dying. It is by your bed, I hope it will give you some comfort, my lady."

"Thank you Cassius," she replied. "Yes, I will go up to my quarters, but I want to go up to see his grave later if you will escort me."

"I will, my lady," he replied, "You need a rest now; I will escort you before dinner is served, if you will allow me."

Lydia followed the housemaid and went into her bedroom with Julia, her maid. She saw he father's letter on the bedside table, turned to Julia and asked her to leave so she could read it in private.

Lydia sat on the bed, opened the letter and began to read. As she read the familiar writing and phrases of her father, her mind travelled back over the years to life at home with the family; her brother, mother, father and friends who always spent time with them. They were such happy times! Her father wrote:

My dearest Lydia

I am most unwell at present, but will pen you a few words before Cassius comes to get me ready for bed. How I appreciate that man! He seems to think for me: he knows me so well after all the years he has been with us. He came to me just when you left for Judea all those years ago, which seems a lifetime. My memories of you are all happy ones. A dutiful and lovely daughter, what more could I ask for?

Now I am expecting to join the ancestors in the near future – life being what it is. I do not know if I will see you again in this world, but I am sure we will meet again somewhere and be together again as family. I am getting very tired now…

From there his writing became indecipherable, but she could just make out his last few words of farewell and his signature.

Putting the letter down, she looked out of the window at the garden – the garden that she remembered he loved so much – and wiped the tears from her eyes. She then turned back to the bed and lay down, overcome by sadness, and with a severe lancing left-sided headache, which gave her a distorted vision, she eventually dozed off to sleep.

She woke up an hour later feeling remarkably refreshed. The headache had abated, she'd never experienced one like that before, but with a determination to get on with life, she was well aware that there was going to be a lot to do. She assumed it would now be her responsibility to run the estate and cope with all the things that life would throw at her. She sat up and noticed that Julia had put away her clothes and jewellery and tidied the room. Looking around her, she noticed that the door was half ajar. She called to her maid, who came in followed by Cassius.

"My lady," he said, "I trust you feel a little more rested now?"

She smiled at him. "Yes indeed. Will you take me now to see my father's grave?"

He bowed to her deferentially. "If you will follow me, my lady, I will do so."

Putting on her shoes and outdoor cloak, she tidied her hair and followed him into the garden. At the top of the small grassy knoll surrounded by cypress trees, with a distant view of the sea, and the fertile fields of her father's estate spreading before her, she stood by her parent's grave. She knelt, and placing a small bunch of flowers on the raised earth, whispered, "Thank you for everything, both of you, and goodbye, until we meet again. I will never forget you."

CHAPTER 4

The following morning, after a restless night in a strange bed, she awoke to what she felt was a very different world, and having broken her fast on honey and eggs, called for Cassius to plan the day ahead. Julia was still fussing about trying to fit in Lydia's belongings, remarking that she had forgotten just how much they'd brought with them from Judea.

Cassius came into the room. "My lady," he said, "your father's lawyer, Claudius, will be arriving before noon; will you see him before or after the midday meal?"

"I'll see him when he arrives. Will he be staying the night?" asked Lydia. "There will be a lot to talk about."

Claudius would arrive early, she knew. Cassius said he was a pleasant man who would greet her politely even in her diminished social state as the wife of a criminal, and also offer his sincere condolences on the death of her father, but Lydia's first priority was to know the fate of her husband. Only when she knew that could she get on with the business of the day. Where was he and what charges had been laid against him? Was he in Rome or had he been sent to a penal colony? She worried that he would be subjected to inhumane treatment; she had heard of the executive's punishment centres and would rather know that her husband was indeed dead, as she feared, than alive and abused. She had few people of consequence to whom she could now turn. Pilate himself had few relations. He was born in Germany, she knew, and his father had died many years ago. He had a brother, but she had no knowledge of him, and there had been no contact with him all the years they were in Judea.

When they were married eight years ago, none of his family had attended the ceremony, only her father and mother, neither of whom were very enamoured with her choice of husband. They considered him to be – they confided to her in a quiet moment at the wedding feast – an unsympathetic man, and felt that his attitude bode ill for the future and for her in particular. But she loved him and he returned that love when they were alone; neither liked a display of emotion in public, and she came to acknowledge that at heart he was a loyal and true friend – even though for a few years life did get a bit difficult when her first pregnancy miscarried, and when she was subsequently unable to conceive the child she knew he desperately wanted. She came to admire his efficiency as procurator, harsh though he was with any dissent; even in one of the most turbulent territories in the empire he had kept the peace – just! When there was insurrection he put it down firmly, but the population came to know what he was like and knew what punishment that would be carried out. He was no more harsh than many Roman leaders at the time, whose word was law; do as you are bidden, or pay, and by the gods you would pay if you were a law breaker. The problem was that this attitude created many enemies for Rome, but Rome did not ask to be loved. There were only three rules: pay your taxes, do as you are told, and obey all the rules!

The trouble in Jerusalem was not a unique occurrence but this time she had known in her heart, and had told

Pilate, so that it would end in tears. And the voice had told her this, not in so many words, but in the way and implication of how it had said it, and indeed trouble had now come.

Although a subject nation, the Jews were a strange people she felt, and their laws, based upon the words of an old prophet who lived centuries ago, claimed that there was only one god, that they were his chosen people, and that this god loved them. They also believed that this god created the world and all that was in it. However, she could never understand why, if their belief was that he was a loving deity, they could be so unkind to their own people as well as anybody else they didn't see eye-to-eye with – ultimately despising anyone who was a non -Jew. They also had the notion that that they would answer to this god when they died, but with these beliefs how could they accept that they would be excused from punishment for despising one of god's creatures – a fellow human being, even though he was not a Jew – when they stood before their judge. From what she had seen of them, she felt that they certainly obeyed the letter of their law, but not the spirit. Not much love there!

She also refuted their claim that a man's illness, however insignificant, was caused by his failure to obey the law, so that ill health was therefore a punishment for what they termed *sin*. This meant that it might not be their own sin that had caused the trouble, but even their father or grandfather's sin. *Not much mercy there either,* she thought. *That is cruel, and they had called her husband harsh!* At least Roman law was straightforward – break the rules, and you were punished – and didn't depend upon any outdated opinion.

All this was going through her mind when Claudius the lawyer arrived and began to set up in the dining room, laying out all his papers, scrolls and writing instruments.

When he was ready, he came to the door and invited Lydia to come in, explaining that he would inform her of the present situation. However, Lydia's first question even before she sat down, was, "Where is my husband and what is happening to him?"

The lawyer at once realised that nothing was going to be done until he could answer that question. He certainly did not have the ear of the president of the court's martial, he told her, but he could possibly make enquiries which could lead to an answer.

She sighed, "Well please get on with it. We'd better postpone this meeting until you have some news." It was not until two days later that he returned to give her as full an account of events as he had found out.

Over the next two days, she found she had little to do; with no authority to influence events – she had to leave the day-to-day running of her father's house to Cassius, and the farms were run by their managers – she had much time to think over her life with Pilate. She thought back to that dreadful day when she miscarried, and Pilate had been so upset that his desire for a son and heir would not be fulfilled. And then she found she was unable to conceive, and a major shadow had been cast over their lives and their future for ever. She knew that infertility was a well-known reason for divorce, but she found that Pilate grieved for her as much as she grieved for herself in her childless state. He was a loyal husband and they just got on with living and loving each other.

She was now in her early thirties, approaching middle age, and knew that if she was to become a widow, there would be little chance of finding another man of Pilate's calibre to marry, and no chnace of having a family. So it would only be for her money, if she was allowed to inherit it, and she could not bear to live with a man who only wanted her money. She would have to resign herself to a lonely life.

That night as she lay down to sleep, after worshipping the household gods in the penetralia (the inner sanctum) and feeling little better for it apart from the fact that her actions were a familiar part of the evening and usually gave her some comfort, she eventually dozed off. Her headache had returned tonight, this time accompanied with a slight feeling of nausea, and in the early morning the voice came to her.

For the first time it spoke to her by name: "Lydia, I'm still here." It paused and she turned her head to listen, now wide awake. "One day you will learn of me to your comfort, but not in this land. Farewell until then."

Then it was gone and she went back to sleep, surprisingly comforted by the thought that she did have a future – irrational as the thought was!

But when she awoke the following morning, she spent the rest of the day trying to find something to do to fill the yawning chasm of her anxiety for the future, which once again had overwhelmed her. Julia, an accomplished singer, played the lute and sang for her mistress, but Lydia got little comfort from this. It only irritated her and she asked her to stop as she preferred the silence. Suddenly after midday, there was a flurry of activity outside and Cassius brought in Claudius and a senator – a man she did not recognize – into the atrium, both looking hot and dishevelled from their apparently hurried journey to the villa from the city. It was a hot day, and in the heat of midday even the birds had stopped singing as the fierce sun beat down on the garden .

"What is it?" she asked, "What has happened? Have you news of my husband?"

Both men bowed to her in greeting. "My lady, we have sad news for you, I'm afraid," replied Claudius. "Your husband is dead, as you feared."

Lydia felt her gut churn. She sat down suddenly in her father's old chair and put her head in her hands. She held up her hand to silence them for a moment, and then when she had recovered a little from the sudden news, said in a strangled voice, "Tell me about it then."

"First, my lady, I must introduce you to my colleague Gratius here. He is another lawyer, and also a senator, but does work mainly for the army." Lydia looked up and nodded to him. "Well go on, what happened?" she asked quietly.

"It was as you feared, my lady," said Gratius. "The procurator had upset an influential man close to the emperor with his outspoken ways, and I'm afraid trumped-up charges were laid against him. In a secret court martial they found him guilty of treason and sentenced him to the quarries in Sicily, or he could choose to take poison and so take his own life because of his exemplary war record. They said the State would give him an honourable funeral, his good name would be preserved and your inheritance from him honoured."

"What a lot of hypocrites!" she said scornfully. "Did he have any chance to answer his accusers?"

"I'm afraid not, my lady," he replied somberly. "It was all done quickly and in virtual secrecy. None of his accusers were in court."

"They should all be ashamed of themselves; not one of them were fit to tie up his sandals," she said angrily.

"Quite so, my lady," said Gratius, "but as a general rule all personal possessions of convicted men go to the state – at least in these circumstances you will still inherit."

"Thank you very much," she replied sarcastically, "So am I supposed to be grateful that they consider my life without my husband is nothing? But giving me a villa and a bit of gold means I should be grateful? I do not think so! It's so obvious what happened: Pilate knew his accuser was up to some wrong doing, and his accuser knew Pilate was aware of it, so my husband had to go. The same old story – it's who you know that counts, and that's Roman justice!"

Neither man looked up: both were studying their feet. Suddenly Gratius said quietly, "A decree has come from the emperor stating his sorrow at the passing of so great a public servant who died in mysterious circumstances. He was an example to us all to the end of his life and he will be sadly missed."

Lydia laughed sardonically. "The howling hypocrites. My husband used to say that the state was bigger than the man – how many times have I heard that!

"Indeed my lady," the senator replied, "but I'm afraid that's life for us Romans. We live on a knife's edge and have to watch our backs constantly."

CHAPTER 5

Two years had passed since the dreadful death of her husband and Lydia was now spending the majority of her time running the estates bequeathed to her by her father, and the property in the capital by her husband. This was a large block of housing near the commercial hub of the city and was proving to be a very lucrative investment indeed. To such an extent that when a poor harvest on the farms was experienced in her second year of ownership, the income from the properties easily made up the financial shortfall with revenue to spare.

On the whole, the two years after the initial shock of her husband's demise were filled with the day-to-day concerns of being a rich business woman, and she went to bed at night tired and often exhausted, but slept well. She had ceased to be bitter about the events of two years ago; it did no good to dwell on it. After all, bitterness on some person's part had caused it to happen, and no amount of worry or bitterness would bring him back.

So she got on with life, changing what needed changing and improving where it was necessary. She had retained Cassius, her father's majordomo; he was getting on a bit but worked well and was content. Julia, her personal maid, was still with her, Gratius a frequent visitor – he was, as was required by law, now her guardian – and Claudius still advised her on tax affairs and legal matters. Her housekeeper had died of a chest infection in her first winter and she employed in her place Mariam, a young but intelligent woman, from the village and trained her in her own way. She had proved to be a wise choice, keeping the house spotless and making sure the household slaves did their duties correctly.

The farms ran well, producing a high standard of crops and a good output, the bills were all paid regularly, the property in the city and the value of the land under the present regime continued to increase in value year on year, and hopefully would continue to do so whilst Emperor Tiberius remained in his post.

All in all, Lydia now experienced a good life. She remained in robust health, had had no more of those awful lancing headaches, and began to view the frustrations of widowhood and the lack of a constant shoulder to cry on with equanimity. She just got on with a life full of work and things to do.

She took more interest in her workers than was usual for a businesswoman of her time. She had a number of slaves, mainly people from the east, but like her father before her she was kind and considerate to them, being aware that they too were human beings and had the same basic needs as herself. After one or two initial incidents, when they tried to take advantage of her good nature, she had had to treat the miscreants firmly and fairly, and they eventually came to repay her attitude with hard work performed to the best of their abilities. So her relationship with her staff was good.

Socially she had resurrected a number of friendships from before she had left with her husband for Judea. Her friends were mainly those who had married well in society, and thanks to Tiberius' decree regarding her husband, few knew the true story of his tragedy. She began to invite her friends, and their husbands and children, to the villa for parties, and the house was often filled with the shouts of children and general laughter. The pool she had built at the back of the villa proved to be very popular with both the children and their parents. Life, for all her past misery, was as good as it could be.

She still worshipped the household gods in the penetralia each evening before bed and gave thanks for another satisfactory day. She never got a lot out of the act of prayer, however, or the spiritual refreshment that she felt she needed, but it was a comfort to repeat the same well-known prayers and phrases each bed time. But she felt there was something missing in her life. She had everything now to make her life comfortable, but this missing something was hard to describe and she could not put her finger on it. She seemed to be waiting for something, but what?

Politically, things were changing. Old Emperor Tiberius died and his grandson Gaius Caligula – known irreverently as 'Little Boots' – was appointed in his place. It was whispered by some that he hastened the old man's demise with the help of a pillow, but initially he was most popular, in particular with the plebs. Eschewing Tiberius' frugality, he bought his popularity with bread and circuses and cancelled the sales tax to get the merchants on his side. But then, when all looked set for a boost in the economy, he fell seriously ill, and for two months it was reputed that he hovered between life and death. He quickly recovered, but his personality and behaviour had changed completely. Some said he had gone mad, and after he thoroughly upset the Senate, he tried to make his horse a consul, and then declared himself a god. He disgusted the Jews by putting a statue of himself in their own Holy of Holies in the worship area of the Temple in Jerusalem. His strange behaviour, it was later reported had been felt throughout the Empire, and people realized it could not continue.

For the business community it was a worrying time, as they wondered where he would get the money from for his extravagant behaviour – many planned to get their fortunes off shore to safer havens. It all created an atmosphere of uncertainty, and Lydia was one of many who feared what would happen if anyone was found to oppose his wishes. However, she simply continued to put all her energies into the businesses and preferred to keep her head down, rarely leaving the estate.

One day, however, her friend Drusilla, from the village across the shallow valley in front of her villa, spent an afternoon with Lydia. Drusilla's husband was an officer in the Praetorian Guard at the palace, and they lived in a large villa about half a mile from Lydia's home. As evening set in, Drusilla said to Lydia, "It's time I went home; walk with me down the drive to the main road and my slave will walk the rest of the way with me."

It was a pleasant evening in which the birds were still singing and the sun was going down over the sea like a large orange ball. A large ocean-going galley was seen standing in toward land. It had a deep red sail, on a sea that was emerald green under a sky now turning red. It made a lovely picture, and made Lydia turn to Drusilla and say, "Just look at that; what a lovely sight! We are so lucky to live in such a beautiful place."

Drusilla stopped and looked with her at the view. She sighed wistfully. "Not quite like home, but almost." Drusilla came from further down the coast where it was mountainous and preferred it to the flatter lands west of Rome.

A tall man with two young boys was also walking along the main road. As they came up to Lydia and Drusilla the man raised his hand in salute and stared hard at Lydia.

"My lady, aren't you the lady Lydia that I met in Judea?" he asked, smiling.

Lydia stared back at him and suddenly recognised him. "Isn't it Centurion Augustus? What a surprise," she said, laughing.

"It is indeed," he said, bowing to her and Drusilla. "It's Tribune Augustus now, but how nice to meet you again after all this time. May I say at once how sorry I was to hear about your husband's passing. The Emperor was most complimentary about him and his work. He was a good officer and will be greatly missed by the general staff."

"Thank you, Tribune," she replied guardedly. "You are most kind, but now I run the estate on my own and it prospers, as you can see, so you must come up to see me with the family. We will have a good chat about old times, the children will enjoy the pool and I've got a couple of very friendly donkeys – the boys will like that. When did you get back to Rome?"

"Oh, a few weeks ago. We like it here, so I shall accept your offer and we'll be in touch. I'll bid you good evening until later this week," and with that he bowed to the two women and walked on with the children.

Drusilla called to her slave, said goodbye to Lydia, waved her hand and walked down the road home. Lydia turned to walk back up the drive to the villa. It was nearly dark now but she knew the driveway well, and walked quickly.

As soon as she got into the villa, she called for Cassius. "I'm going to bed now, will you send Julia to me?" she asked him.

Julia arrived quickly. "Will you take your warm drink before you go up, Madame?" she said. "It's a long time since you last ate and you won't sleep if you are hungry."

Lydia smiled at her.

"Oh, Julia, what would I do without you? You think for me, don't you!"

Julia smiled, pleased at the compliment, and went to fetch the drink of warm goat's milk flavoured with Lydia's favourite herbs.

After Lydia had drunk her milk, she went upstairs to the bedroom and with Julia's help had a bath and then got into bed. She stretched herself and settled into the comfort of the newly washed bedding, which was the finest silk sheets she could get. Glancing out of the window, she saw that the moon was just showing over the hills to the west, bathing the landscape in its silvery light. She could just hear the roar of the city; had it not been for that it would have been perfect.

But even as she relaxed she realized that though she was surrounded by luxury and had everything she could possibly ask for, a hole was still there in her life. She missed her husband and a familiar shoulder to cry on. She certainly did not want to be married again, and was well aware that as she was infertile, any man would only marry her for her money. She had met a lot of men like that, but to live with someone whose only thought was to use her for her fortune was repellent. Anyway, no man could possibly come up to the standard of Pilate – that she knew – and with those thoughts she went to sleep.

Next morning after breakfast, a messenger arrived with a message from Tribune Augustus, asking if it would be possible for him to bring his two boys with him that afternoon for a visit. He'd told them about the pool and they were very excited at the prospect of a swim. His wife was visiting her mother who was ill so she would be unable come. Lydia was delighted, she loved the company of children, and told the messenger that she would be looking forward to the visit with the greatest pleasure.

Giving instructions to Mariam, her housekeeper, she asked her if she knew what young boys liked to eat. "Oh yes, Madame," she laughed. "I have two young brothers myself and am well aware of boys' likes and dislikes."

"Right," replied Lydia."Well I'll leave it to you to arrange the meal; we'll have it on the patio by the pool. They'll be here mid-afternoon so you've plenty of time to get ready. By the way, their father, Tribune Augustus, will also be with them and staying for the afternoon."

The family arrived and the meal was served as planned. The boys spent more time in the pool than out of it, and after the meal, as the tribune and Lydia relaxed, they indulged in small talk for a time. Then suddenly Augustus asked her if she remembered the story he had told her about his sick servant who had been healed in Caesarea by the travelling preacher.

"Indeed I do," she replied. "He did a lot of good work

for the locals, I believe. How dreadful that his own people hated him enough to kill him. It still makes me sad to think of it. My husband told me he was no charlatan, but somehow he offended the Temple people. I just couldn't understand it, when as you know, there were so many charlatans peddling their wares at that time."

She went on to tell him of the morning of that extraordinary day, but then paused for a moment and shook her head. Augustus looked at her quizzically. "Yes, my lady?" he asked quietly. She forced herself out of her thoughts, and suddenly found herself telling him about her dream the night before the trial, and the voice that had spoken to her. Lydia was surprised at how easy she found it was to talk to this man. He listened carefully to all she said, occasionally asking a question and making a well-considered comment.

"I cannot imagine why they should kill such a good man. He was only looking after those people that they should have been caring for," she said quietly. "Why did they do it?"

Augustus thought for a moment, choosing his words with care. "He was a preacher primarily, but his message was like a fire which would have burnt up all their cherished ideas and ideologies, and that meant he was a danger to their very existence."

"In what way? she asked.

"He once said, I was told, that a very rich man who'd made his fortune by nefarious means came to see him. He had heard this man preach and realised that he was in danger of losing his very soul in the pursuit of money – and also the tax people were after him, which was probably a more powerful motive!

"He asked if he could join his followers and the preacher said to him, 'By all means, but sell everything you possess and give the proceeds to the poor. Your treasure is nowhere near as valuable as the treasure I will give you, which is peace of mind, contentment, happiness and the joy of living a full life without any selfish motive. All this you will get if you treat your neighbour in the same way as you would like to be treated yourself. Will you do this?' And the poor chap went away sad because the price was too high for him. So if the Jewish hierarchy were to do the same they would loose all the trappings of power and cease to function. They didn't want to be loved or to love, like all despots they wanted to stay in power, whoever got hurt. It wasn't that the preacher had done anything wrong, but what got up the hierarchy's noses was that their power base depended upon control of their subjects, and an idea like that was destructive to their comfort."

"Hmm," said Lydia, "I see what you mean. Oh I'd have loved to have met him. Perhaps that was his voice that spoke to me. He must have been an exceptional man, it was obvious by the way he spoke."

"He had a remarkably compelling voice," replied Augustus thoughtfully. "You could almost hear the sunshine in it."

Lydia smiled and nodded her head. "Yes, I know what you mean," she said.

He continued, "But he was no weakling, you know. He took on a lot of his critics and usually confounded them!"

Lydia smiled and nodded her head again. "Yes, I believe so," she said. "What happened to his followers then?"

"When I left, they were getting their act together I believe. They were convinced he was still alive. I couldn't quite make it out, maybe it was wishful thinking, but one of their leaders claimed he had spoken to him. They are calling him the promised Messiah, the Son of God – which god I don't know, the Jewish one I assume. They call him Yahweh I believe. The mainstream lot were always banging on about their Messiah who would come one day and rescue them from all forms of tyranny and subjection, and make them great again in the world as they had been centuries before. This new movement which claims he is still alive and says he is the Messiah has really upset the Temple. The trouble is, so far as the hierarchy are concerned his message of caring for the poor and loving your neighbour didn't quite equate with their idea of what a Messiah should be like, they want a warrior, so they ganged up on him – hence his execution. But looking at their leaders, they are nothing more than greedy and selfish sycophants and toadies. I'm sure your husband would have had little respect for people like them. He was too honest a man for that."

"True," said Lydia thoughtfully, "but if there are enough toadies and sycophants, it provides a real and present danger in any state. We've got enough of them!"

"I think you're right," he replied, "and I'm glad to be out of it. It didn't affect me a lot as a serving soldier, but I saw the amount of misery caused to a number of his followers by that execution. To be quite honest, and don't quote me on this, it was judicial murder in my opinion. Politics and politicians disgust me!"

Lydia was so relieved to have had the opportunity to talk about her feelings regarding the voice – it was cathartic to do so, having had nobody in the past that she felt she could open up to.

After this the afternoon went very quickly. The children had a great time in the pool and on the donkeys, under the benevolent eye of Cassius. "Lovely kids," he remarked to Lydia when they had gone, with a promise of more fun when they came again at a later date.

So once again the house was empty of laughter and children's noises, but later, after her evening meal, and as she relaxed in her father's chair in the atrium, Cassius announced the arrival of Gratius on one of his monthly visits. Although Lydia had come to value his friendship, and they were now on first-name terms, she could never have the conversation with him that she had had with the tribune. However, he brought news of the new emperor's damaging attack on some businessmen in the city. To get his hands on their properties he had, it was said, levelled false charges of treason against them, and in a closed session had had two men executed so he could appropriate their land and property for his own use. He looked very grave as he recounted the news to Lydia and went on to tell her of the emperor's attitude to the Senate, which was one of contempt. Furthermore he had declared himself divine, threatening anyone who disputed this – and to cap it all had told the Senate he was definitely going to make his horse consul!

"So what are we going to do, and why is he doing this?" asked Lydia. "What would I do if all this was stolen from me by that thug?"

"Well, we will have to pre-empt him before he gets the opportunity to do it, Lydia," he replied. "You could realise your assets in the city, take the gold and invest elsewhere."

Lydia looked at him, frowning. "But that property in the city is an excellent source of income, and supplements the farm when we get a lean year as we did last year. And what of my poor staff? If I sold up, they would be on the streets with no income. I've got five managers there, each with a wife and children to feed, I couldn't bear to see them destitute."

"Why do you think like that, Lydia?" he queried. "You're a business woman and workers are two a penny – that's the way of the world!"

"My father didn't see people like that," she retorted, "and neither do I, I think people matter. Obviously Rome doesn't care about its citizens, but I do. These are the people who work for us and make our money, are we just to throw them away? Were it not for them, there would be no viable business."

Gratius looked at her quizzically. "You're ahead of your time, Lydia," he said. "I don't think I've heard of anybody else who considers their workers like that."

"Well I've got my father's blood in me," she replied with a degree of asperity, "and he did concern himself with others, it's why they worked so well for him and made all you see around you. It didn't just happen you know!"

They continued to chat for a few minutes until it was time for him to go. "I'll see you in a few days and let you know what is happening," he said, putting on his coat. "But I can see nothing good on the horizon with this man in charge. We will just have to keep our heads down and hope it blows over. He will probably overreach himself like all tyrants and somebody will get him. But until then we must keep our ears open and be ready to react."

Gratius arrived a few days later in a hurry. Without bothering with the niceties, he began, "Lydia, there is a rumour, I don't know if it is true, but I heard it from a reliable source that the emperor is sending visiting commissioners to all landowners. He is trying to wrong-foot them by asking the landowner for their opinion regarding the emperor's divinity, and if you give the wrong impression, beware! As I say, it's a rumour , but there is rarely smoke without fire. He will treat a wrong answer as treason."

"Oh dear, where will it all end?" she replied in a worried voice.

"Yes," replied Gratius, "where indeed!"

After he left, Lydia, having had a very busy and worrying day, went to bed, but her mind was in turmoil. Augustus' reminiscences of the other afternoon had taken her back to her life by the lake, but now Gratius' news meant that the life she had looked forward to, and which she thought she was achieving, was in tatters.

She dozed off, then suddenly sat up with a jerk. "I'm getting out of here for the time being," she said. "I'll go and find out about that voice, back in Judea, then when I return, this should all have blown over. I'll arrange it with Gratius tomorrow," and with that she fell fast asleep.

CHAPTER 6

The wind was set fair and the ship's captain declared it the best sailing weather he'd seen for weeks. There were three months to go before winter set in, when no safe travel was possible on the Mare Nostrum and all sailing had to cease. As the big corbitas – the cargo and passenger vessels of the Roman merchant navy – sailed out of the strait between the toe of Italy and the island of Sicily, later to be named the Strait of Messina, the westerly winds filled the sails. They forced the prow of the vessel deep into the blue waves that had powered their way from the Pillars of Hercules far to the west.

Lydia sat in the captain's cabin at the stern of the vessel. She enjoyed sailing and this was to be the journey of a lifetime for her; an escape back to Tiberius to find her mystery voice, and to see her old friends again.

The coast of Italy slipped away to the port side, and they were soon alone on the great and lonely expanse of the ocean. The strange feeling Lydia had of complete safety was extraordinary. She had initially viewed the prospect of this voyage with apprehension, travelling with her maid Julia and Alexander, a young kinsman of Gratus who he had insisted she took as a guard. However, she now felt she was following her star, as her old aunt Aurelia used to say; this was her destiny, and she looked forward with confidence to each day as it came.

There were also a large number of passengers on board, mainly military personnel and their wives, destined for Antiochus in the northern part of the Tetrarchy, but she kept to her own part of the ship so that she could live with her thoughts. She had much to think about . In the last few months and years so much had happened!

The vessel left its military passengers at Antiochus and replenished food and water there. It then proceeded along the coast into quieter waters to Caesarea, where she and her companions would disembark. The ship would be going on to Alexandria to take on board a cargo of grain destined for the voracious appetite of the huge city of Rome, which needed a huge amount of food to maintain the many slaves it had acquired, and due to it's urbanisation. This also kept the emperor in favour with the plebs, who constantly needing placating to keep the Pax Romana at home. As many as five shiploads a day were required for this, and more to go into store for the winter months when no ships could be put to sea.

She was surprised that it had been possible to get the ship to divert to Caesarea. The vessel would load grain at its final port of call, Alexandria, but Gratus quoted the name of Lydia's late husband to the ship owner, and straightaway the route was changed. *Not what you know*, thought Lydia, *but who you know*!

The journey had been expected to last some twenty days, but having had such favourable weather for the last two weeks, they were almost there. It had been an incident-free journey, the threat of piracy was still there but much less than it had been before Pompey and

Julius Caesar had handed out tough medicine to the pirates caught interfering with Rome's food supplies – they were not inclined to be given another dose. Lydia had spent a lot of the time in thought, reading, looking at the sea or indulging in small talk with Julia and Alexander. She thought back to the last few weeks when the threat of being hounded by the Emperor's men had been a reality, and she had lived in fear and dread of an unannounced arrival. It was said to often happen at night, with demands for hospitality and the certain interrogation to follow. These people were all security service men trained in the art of questioning and would expose your thoughts as easy as a robin pulling a worm out of its hole. Before you knew it, you had divulged your innermost doubts and opinions.

However, she had avoided this thanks to Gratius, who had diverted them away from her villa by some means, and spirited her by stage coach to Ostia and onto the grain ship. It had been a hair-raising few hours, but she was now well away from it all, and the voyage had been balm for her troubled soul.

So after a peaceful voyage, the ship arrived one afternoon at Caesarea, where the new docks had been built to accommodate the largest vessels. After it had been tied up, Lydia and her companions were able to walk off the ship – unlike in lesser ports in this part of the Empire, where disembarking required a ferry to take you to shore. She was immediately greeted by the garrison's movement officer, who was the man she remembered from her departure from this same dock three years before.

"My lady," he said, smiling, "this is a pleasant

surprise. Is there anything I can do for you? I had no idea you would be coming."

"Thank you, Centurion," she replied. "When the crew have unloaded my luggage, my companions and I will need transport to Tiberius. I know I am no longer the wife of a serving officer, but if you would arrange it I will pay you in advance."

Centurion Albinus immediately sent a messenger to the garrison commander with a message regarding her requirements and said, "But you are the wife of a very famous officer, my lady, a fine man that even the Emperor was pleased to recognise, and rightly so. I was an admirer of your husband and was so sad to hear of his death. It was a great loss to the army, if I may say so. The very least I can do is to help you on your way."

The garrison commander arrived and was equally complimentary, offering her hospitality until transport and their escort was ready. He arranged for a fast courier to be sent to Procurator Marcellus at the palace at Tiberius, announcing their arrival three days hence. He explained to her that there would be an armed escort provided, because the terrorist group the Zealots had been active in the area of late and it was necessary to ensure Lydia and her companions' safety on the three-day journey.

Lydia was overwhelmed by the kindness of these officers, and so grateful to be under the protection of military men again. They were organized, straight talking and completely trustworthy, unlike most of the civilian administration at home, who she had come to view with contempt as self-serving and corrupt.

So three days after their interesting and incident-free journey, she came in sight of the lake again. As they breasted the slight hill on the road, below her she saw the familiar and beautiful sight of the lake just as she remembered it, with gardens full of flowers along its shore and the sailing and fishing boats with their many coloured sails bent to the wind as they proceeded on their way across the water.

"How beautiful," she murmured to Julia.

"Indeed, Madame, what a pity human beings always ruin things!" Julia replied.

It was with relief that they had arrived safely at the lakeside, having been told that there were bandits at work in the area.

The journey this time had been quite an education for her and her companions. The journey down to Caesarea three years before with her husband had been a stately affair, with all the trappings of power on display. They had been accompanied by a massive cavalry escort then, compared with the four troopers provided for her this time in her civilian capacity – these were only allowed because she was known to the garrison commander at the port of Caeserea.

She had seen little of the countryside on the previous journey, or its people, who on the whole were intimidated by the show of force and so kept away. Thinking about it though, she hadn't wanted to see them, being only interested in getting to the ship. But this time as they passed through the small villages, consisting by and large of hovels and rudimentary shelters, she now saw the local population who came out in curiosity to see them pass by.

She had lived for the last years in either palaces or

great country estates in Rome, Jerusalem or Tiberius. Brought up with a silver spoon in her mouth, she was now appalled to see such poverty, disease and malnutrition, the extent of which she would never have imagined possible in the Empire. She thought that if ever there was a group of people who needed help – the sort of help that the preacher she had heard of had given to them, which provided some sort of expectation in life and allowed them to raise their heads a little above ground level, possibly giving a little hope or aid with their diseases – these were the ones. The children all appeared to be stunted, malnourished and often disfigured with disease. They looked dirty, with running noses and flies crawling in and out of their eyes and ears, but considering the way the few rich people around treated them, with such utter contempt, it was understandable they were like this.

The troop commander advised her not to stop, no matter how heartrending it was to see, as they were a dirty, feckless and thieving lot. It was the lepers who were saddest group; they walked together in small parties, ringing a bell and calling "Unclean" as they went by. They would, the officer said, starve to death unless food was put out for them, and most did die of starvation. Leprosy was a death sentence if you caught it, and you were avoided by all.

She had little knowledge of the hoi polloi at home because of her background, she had never come in contact with many, but when she had, there did not seem to be the same level of degradation that she found here. Nobody would help these people! So this journey had been quite a shock to her and her companions: beggars everywhere, diseased with multiple deformities, it had been most unpleasant spectacle. A nation which needed a Messiah indeed – not a warrior king, but a saviour from their poverty of pocket, mind, body, spirit and disease.

Even at home, health was maintained on a knife's edge. She had heard of the dreadful effect of smallpox, plague and measles, which cost thousands of lives a year. Life was precarious, so was it not possible for governments to put aside their desire of pursuing wealth and conquest for once, and spend some of their ill–gotten gains on trying to solve the problems of poverty and disease?

But here in Palestine, the Jews, who were the majority faith, considered that all these woes of mankind were the result of personal sin – that is, as she recalled, the breaking of the law of one of their ancient prophets, who had received the law from their god. One law was not to steal, so if you had no food or were unable to get work to provide for your family, and you stole food, you would therefore be guilty of law breaking – and their god would punish you with ill health. Is this what they called justice and mercy? So it was your own fault if you became ill, lame or deformed, and their leaders had executed the only man who had ever tried to help! She was not surprised that the people followed him in crowds, all hoping for something better in their lives.

Rome had at least tried to bring some sort of order to this country, but in reality, as she had seen, the Jews did not want it, and the main beneficiary of this order was the Greek and Roman immigrants, and the occupiers of the country who came in after Pompey's invasion all those years ago.

Alexander was horrified at what he had seen. Like Lydia, he had been brought up in luxury, as the grandson of a senator and the son of a rich landowner, and he recoiled in horror at some of the sights. But unlike Lydia he had little pity for them, only contempt; he could not see why they should not be treated the way they were treated, and agreed with the troop commander that they were a feckless lot who were not worth worrying about. Lydia was upset by his attitude and remarked that little did he realise how fortunate he was in his upbringing, and to live in a civilised city like Rome. Hopefully, maybe, he would learn to be grateful for his many blessings; he had everything he wanted, yet they had nothing, even their basic needs were never met. As his grandfather Gratius had remarked to Lydia, she was before her time – a remark that still rankled with her – but she knew that there was such a thing as natural justice. One day, if and when Rome was brought to its knees, Rome too would learn this, and if their present emperor continued with his behaviour, this could be soon!

Her musings over, she saw that they were now approaching the palace. At the portico they were met by the guard on duty, who had been given instructions to have them escorted to their quarters. He then informed the unit commander of the arrival of the party at the palace.

CHAPTER 7

Lydia awoke the next morning to a cold, blustery and damp world. Winter would soon arrive with its sudden storms which made the lake dangerous for sailors and the fishermen. She yawned as she opened her eyes and suddenly remembered that the voice had spoken to her again during the night for the first time in weeks, just as it had promised her the last time she had experienced it, she was indeed in another land now.

She concentrated her mind to recall its message. "Only give to Caesar what is his." "But what in heaven's name does that mean?" she said out loud, realizing that she had another riddle to answer. The only thing Caesar wanted were his taxes, collected without mercy from everybody. *He doesn't give anything back,* she thought, cynically.

A blast of rain splattered against the shutters of her room. She shivered and sank back into the warmth of the bedclothes and dozed off again, until she heard Julia call from outside her room, "Are you awake, Madame? Your bath will be ready in a short while."

Breakfast, served by a slave, was eaten in the dining room off the atrium. Alexander and she sat in companionable silence as they ate their food, Alexander, excited at the prospect of meeting the procurator, and Lydia still puzzling over her message received in the early hours.

After breakfast, as the dishes were cleared away, Julia was helping Lydia adjust her day gown when the secretary knocked on the door and came into the room. He looked curiously at Lydia and a smile of recognition spread over his face.

"Of course," he exclaimed, "its lady Lydia, I didn't think it would be you. How very nice to see you. The boss will be so pleased to see you again. May I say how very sorry we were to hear of the passing of your husband. He was a fine man, wonderful officer and his death was a great loss to the army. The Emperor, I understand, was effusive in his praise of him."

Poor Lydia had heard it all before, but replied politely. "How very kind, thank you" – *if only they knew,* she thought, *it would be so different!*

"The procurator didn't realize it was you who would be arriving when we got the message," he continued. "We were told it was a friend of Senator Gratius. As soon as I can get in to see him, I'm sure he will see you at once. May I ask the purpose of your visit, or is that confidential?"

"No, it's not confidential. I had to get away from Rome for a time, I now run all my late father's estates and a large investment in the city," she replied. "As a very busy businesswoman, it is tiring on one's own, so I've left it all in the more than capable hands of Senator Gratius."

"Ah, I see," he replied. "So, my lady, I'll tell the boss and I'm sure he will see you immediately," and with that he bowed and left the room to find Procurator Marcellus in his office.

Alexander was impressed. "His secretary is a tribune!" He exclaimed admiringly.

"Well, the procurator is a representative of the emperor, which is just a little lower than the gods," she laughed.

The secretary returned almost at once. "If you will follow me, my lady, we will go over to the office where the boss is waiting for you. He turned to Alexander. "If you will wait here, young man, I'll talk to you in a moment."

Lydia was ushered into the presence of the procurator, who was Pilate's replacement of three years ago. *He looks like Pontius,* she thought, *tall and commanding!* He came from behind his desk smiling to welcome her.

"Lydia," he said laughing, "how very nice to see you again after all this time." He took her hands in his. "By all that's wonderful, this is a surprise! I expected a representative from Senator Gratius, not yourself. How are you? So sorry to hear the bad news about your husband – great loss to the army, he was a fine soldier." *Oh dear,* she thought, *here we go again!*

They exchanged small talk for a while about family matters. Marcellus had lost his wife from some infection just after they arrived to take over from her husband. He also had a son who was in the army campaigning in Germany at present – he had reported well when he last heard of him a month ago. Then after all the mundane matters had been discussed, he looked at her quizzically and asked, "Can you tell me why we are honoured with this visit?"

"It's a long story, Marcellus," she replied, "and it all started in Jerusalem four years ago. It will take a while to tell, have we time?"

"Oh yes, please go on," he replied.

She began to tell him about the way Pilate had handled a difficult situation with the Jewish authorities, and the eventual execution of a man called Jesus of Nazareth.

"It worried me because my husband found him innocent of their charges, but his own people wanted him dead because he had called them liars and hypocrites in public. They never forgave him – and from what I have heard about them, he was quite correct in his estimation of their behaviour." She looked down at her hands, and paused, before frowning.

"Yes, go on, I heard about that case," said Marcellus somewhat puzzled, "but what does that have to do with you specifically?"

"Please don't think me too superstitious," she went on, "but I had feeling about it all before he was executed, I begged my husband to let him go, but these dreadful people were intent on killing him, so he washed his hands of the case. It wasn't Roman law after all, it was a theological dispute. I ask you, killing somebody just because of an unproven idea! I told him it would end in tears, and I think it did."

Marcellous still looked puzzled. "But hundreds of criminals are put to death every year, what is so special about this episode?" he asked.

"I feel I need to find out what really happened," she replied. "I've heard more about him since from those who have come back to Rome from Judea, and so far as I can find out, all he ever did was look after those in need and heal the sick. There is no law in Rome to tell you what you must or must not believe, or that you must not help those in need, is there? At least there wasn't until Caligula became emperor!"

"True, I've heard the emperor has gone mad, or so it is said," he replied. "If so he will not be in that position long if he upsets the Senate too much – somebody will get him! But to get back to your story, what was it that this Jesus said to upset the Jewish authorities apart from calling them hypocrites?"

"Marcellus," said Lydia, thoughtfully, "his message was what my father believed in: forget the religious philosophy, just care for those less fortunate than yourselves. The authorities didn't like that because they had to be top dog all of the time. I find that even in business, if you look after the workers and slaves – and after all, they are the ones who earn your money for you – they will respond by doing a good job. That's a simple enough message surely. So they didn't want that, it troubled what little conscience they had! So they killed him, with a little bit of help from us, but I know my husband was furious with them. There was threat of civil unrest, so he let them get on with it for the sake of the Pax Romana."

"Lydia," said Marcellus, "there must be more to this than you are prepared to divulge." He looked at her carefully. "Do you want to tell me? It'll be confidential after all."

She realised she was not just talking to a soldier who saw things in black and white. She looked down at her hands for a minute, but eventually looked up and told him about the voice and the spectre in her dreams.

"Ah, now I see," he said thoughtfully, "you want to get at the truth. Well it's no good going to their authorities. You'll have to find his erstwhile friends and see what the story is now. I have heard rumblings about a Jewish movement called 'The Way'. They've caused no trouble, you'll probably need to start there." He paused for a moment. "I can't give you any direct support for obvious reasons. I can't take sides as my job is to keep the peace, but will see if there is any way I can help. I think you are asking too much of people to accept your theories though, you are a bit ahead of your time."

Lydia smiled. "Yes, that's what Gratius said," she replied, "but I would like to talk to his friends. I know that will be difficult as a Roman and a woman, but Gratius' grandson Alexander is with me and can help me with that, if he is willing to do so."

"You will need to be very careful and not offend too many sensibilities or your life will be in danger," said Marcellus. "I can get my secretary to place a couple of security men in your vicinity whenever you are out and about, but you know the attitude to women in this country. They are quite ancient in their beliefs, and are also very devious and crafty. I think on reflection you should stay here a few days and I will see how the land lies.

"I shall get my secretary to have a talk with that young man of yours, I don't want him creating a diplomatic incident, nor do I want the grandson of a leading senator in trouble on my patch. So leave it with me and we will have a chat later, but you must excuse me now. I'm in court this morning, so goodbye until dinner this evening."

Lydia spent the next two days relaxing at the palace in Tiberius. Alexander appeared to have been taken under the wing of Tribune Aurelius, the procurator's secretary, and was full of excitement, not only from being in with such a senior officer, but because also, to his delight, he had been introduced to the procurator, who had spent time with Alexander discussing military matters, and Alexander was now convinced that his future lay in the army. Tribune Aurelius had a long conversation with Alexander about his role guarding lady Lydia, and having ascertained that he was fluent in all common languages, gave him a short lesson in Aramaic, the local language. It was not that he was likely to have any in – depth conversations with the locals, it was sufficient for him to learn the simple words for hello, goodbye, good morning, please and thank you and so on. He would be showing an interest in the common people – who were likely to be put off if this well-dressed young Roman, with his expensive accoutrements, could not even say that!

On one of his forays into the town, Alexander had gone to the quayside and watched the fishing boats return with their catch. He was sitting on the quay and got into conversation with an official-looking man of middle age who introduced himself as the local tax gatherer, Zacheus by name. They chatted of this and that, and after a remark by Alexander at the apparent cheerfulness and hard work of the men, Zacheus informed Alexander of the fishing cooperative that had been established in this port. He explained that because the fishing fleet was owned by the men, they worked hard and were now quite prosperous . He said the palace took a lot of their catches and the rest was transported to the capital by daily mule train, providing the men with a good living.

"That sounds a good idea," remarked Alexander, "how did that come about?"

Zacheus went on to tell him of the local preacher whose teachings had encouraged his son–in–law to hand over the whole of his substantial inheritance to the men, which included many properties, to make their lives very much better than it could have been when they worked for a wage, and when the weather was bad and there was no fishing, or the fishing season was over and their families had hardly enough food with which to feed the children. This cooperative had saved many from despair and malnourishment. However, the preacher had fallen out with the authorities in the capital, and they had arrested and executed him.

"What did they do that for?" asked Alexander in astonishment. "He was only trying to help the poor; he must have been quite a man to do this."

"Well he didn't actually do it himself, but his teachings encouraged everyone to care for their neighbour, and that's what happened!"

"Did you meet him?" asked Alexander.

Zacheus replied softly, "Yes I did, and he changed my life completely. He was quite a man, as you said…"

The conversation came to an abrupt end when one of the fishermen had an accident as he was unloading a box of fish. The rope of the crane snapped, and the box fell and hit the man's head, causing it to bleed profusely. Alexander helped the fishermen to stem the flow of blood from the wounded man, then looking at the position of the sun, realised it was time to go. He said goodbye to the men, thanked Zacheus for his time and asked if he could come and talk with him again.

Zacheus said he would like to do that and they said farewell.

Alexander walked away up the hill back to the palace and thought over what the taxman had told him, thinking that lady Lydia would be interested as a businesswoman in this strange tale of cooperation in the work place. *I must tell her about this*, he mused, as he walked along.

That evening the procurator had invited Lydia and Alexander to join him at dinner, and after a good meal washed down with a most refreshing wine, Alexander recounted the conversation he'd had at the quayside with Zacheus.

Lydia listened carefully and remarked, "Yes, that's what I have heard of this preacher. He influenced a lot of people to do things for others, so this sounds typical of the things I've heard."

Marcellus turned to Alexander. "You say that this was told you by this tax man; you know I've heard of his reputation, and for a taxman he's much admired."

"A lot of people passing spoke to Zacheus, sir, he did appear to be popular," replied Alexander.

Marcellus looked at Lydia and smiled. "There you are then, he sounds like a good contact. He must be somebody special for people to like a taxman." He laughed. "They usually hate their guts! Do you think this voice of yours is something to do with the preacher he was on about?"

"I don't know, but that's where it all started," she said, thoughtfully.

"What voice?" asked Alexander.

"I'll tell you tomorrow if you will take me to meet this Zacheus," she said.

Zacheus' house was behind his office on the quayside, and at mid-morning the following day, Lydia and Alexander arrived to talk with him. Alexander knocked on the door, which was opened by Zacheus' servant, who went to find his master.

Eventually, Zacheus came out and said, "Hello, Alexander, what can I do for you?"

"Would you talk to lady Lydia from the palace?" Alexander asked him.

"What does she want?" said Zacheus. "Who is she?"

"I told her about the cooperative fishing fleet, and she is very interested. She is a very rich businesswoman from Rome," replied Alexander.

"Oh well, I suppose we'd better not upset the palace. You'd better show her in, but stay with us while we talk," said Zacheus.

Alexander went out to her. "He will see you, my lady, but wants me to stay with him while he talks to you."

"I understand," she said, "let's go in then."

Zacheus looked at her curiously as Lydia and Alexander came in, he wasn't used to entertaining high – born Roman women. "Come into my office, my lady," he said courteously, "please sit down." He offered her the most comfortable chair in his rather sparsely furnished office. "What can I do for you?"

Lydia began, "I don't know what Alexander here has told you," she gestured toward her young companion, "but what I want to know is how you or your friend were persuaded to develop this idea of what you call a cooperative venture and by whom."

"Why do you ask?" asked Zacheus. "It is most unusual that a Roman citizen, and with all due respect a woman, should be interested in anything we locals do."

"I understand your problem," Lydia said, "but are you prepared to talk to me? I mean you no harm and this conversation would be in confidence; I will divulge nothing of it to the procurator or his staff."

"So long as the conversation is in confidence, yes I will, but I cannot see how a business in Judea can have any bearing on Rome's affairs. All your compatriots want from us are our taxes, which I gather in of course." He smiled.

"Are you prepared to listen to me first?" she asked. "Because my interest goes beyond business, believe me. I can understand your hesitance, but as I said, it is not about the business, but why you formed this cooperative."

"I see," said Zacheus. "Well, we formed it to give the fisher folk a better life, to give them a regular income without being laid-off when the weather was too rough for fishing, and to give them security when the fishing season was over and most of them found it impossible to feed their families."

"Yes," she said, "I can appreciate that, but my question is not what you did, but why you did it. The idea in modern business is unique."

"I'm sorry, my lady," said Zacheus,"but I still cannot understand why you, a Roman, should be in the slightest bit interested in the way we treat our workers."

Lydia thought for a moment, then said quietly, "My late father left me all his businesses, and I manage these according to his principles. He believed that if you treat your people fairly, and with consideration, realising that they are the ones who make your money, you not only get a more efficient business, but you also get the pleasure of their approval of you as the owner – in the same way as a loving, caring father is loved by his children and gets the best for them, and from them."

Zacheus' eyebrows shot up. "Whatever made him be like that?" he whispered. "That behaviour in this day and age is unbelievable. You say he's dead now?" she nodded. "And he was allowed to do this by the authorities?" asked Zacheus, wide-eyed.

"Roman rule is just, so long as you pay your taxes and behave yourself," she replied sardonically. "So long as you comply, there is no need for the authorities to interfere."

Zacheus turned to Alexander . "Did you tell lady Lydia about the preacher whose influence caused us to do this?" he asked.

"I did," he replied, "but I know nothing more than that – you didn't tell me anything further."

"Well, the previous procurator did interfere and asked for more than taxes, and he was the one who killed the preacher Jesus," said Zacheus with a sigh. "Are we supposed to admire Rome then?"

Lydia looked straight at him. "No, he did not kill him," she said firmly, "it was his own people who did that. I begged Pilate to have nothing to do with it, or it would end in tears, and it did."

Zacheus looked startled and went red, "You begged him?" he spluttered.

"Yes I begged him. He was my husband and he was got at by the Sanhedrin. They killed him – true Pilate provided the execution party, but it was the Sanhedrin who killed him."

"So you know all about it then," stammered Zacheus.

"Yes," replied Lydia, "I had a dream and if I may I will tell you about it..." She proceeded to tell him about the voice that had followed her, and how she felt she must find out about it. "...because I think he was more than just a poor preacher from Nazareth. Will you now tell me what I want to know?" she pleaded.

Zacheus looked down at his hands, shook his head, sighed and looked at her. "I think I can better do that," he said, "but I shall have to start at the beginning."

Lydia smiled. "That would be a good place to start." she replied.

CHAPTER 8

A column of horses and their riders were getting near to the capital after two tiring days on the road. The countryside was hardly inspiring; it was hot and dusty, the few trees wilting in the heat. It appeared to be a deserted landscape and the few locals who took the trouble to observe the passing column of Roman officials and armed guards kept their distance – in fear of any abuse if they got in the way, and for their lives if they attempted to interfere with the armed men to any degree. The troopers were not averse to hitting or killing anybody who got too near them; they knew the tactics of the Zealots and were always on the alert for suspicious-looking people who might pull a knife on them at any time. On the whole the column had travelled with little to hinder it. Even the pye–dogs avoided them, and those animals were always going to chance their luck when they thought there might be food to pick up!

Lydia and Alexander were tired. They'd stopped last night near Jericho at a government rest house, which had not been the most salubrious of residences, but it was adequate, but they were now saddle–sore. They would be glad to get to the palace and have a bath and a decent meal, instead of the trooper's rations they'd had since leaving Tiberius.

Lydia thought back to the reason for the journey. Zacheus had eventually, and with some reluctance, recounted the story of the cooperative managed by his son-in-law Reuben, but still seemed very suspicious of her motives, even though she had again promised confidentiality. He had, however, inadvertently given her the name of a senior member of the government who was sympathetic to Zacheus' own principles and who might be persuaded to give her the information she needed. So when Marcellus' secretary told Lydia that a detail of troopers would be leaving Tiberius the next morning with dispatches for the capital, she asked if she could go with them to continue her quest in Jerusalem. In this way she felt she might well get the answers she desperately needed.

The previous night in her room at the rest house, she had gone to bed and slept until the early hours, but had then been awoken again by the voice. It had called her by name and said, "Lydia, you will find my friends." *Is that all it's going to tell me?* she had thought, though it did at least confirm she was on the right road to finding out! The last time it had called her and talked about tax and Caesar, the message had lead to Zacheus – but who were his friends, and how was she to find them? Zacheus had mentioned in passing the name of a man who was a lawyer he knew, a great friend called Nicodemus. Maybe he was the contact she needed.

Suddenly there was a lot of shouting at the head of the column, which had come to a halt as a number of men on mules got in the way. They were herding a group of manacled and dishevelled men, women and children along, beating them every now and then across the shoulders with whips as they cried out pitifully in protest. They looked a sad lot and the troop commander shouted at the leader to get out of the way.

"What are you doing with those people?" he shouted to their guard.

The leader of the group, a short, bald, bearded man said he was taking them to prison for committing blasphemy and heresy.

"On whose orders?" asked the troop commander.

The man relied archly, "On the orders of my friend the High Priest. This is no more than they deserve; they deserve to die, and probably will."

Lydia heard the cruelty in the man's voice, turned on him and said, "Why are you so cruel? They're exhausted, look at them, they need a rest."

He sneered at her. "What do you know about it? You Romans are just as cruel," he snarled, "They're my prisoners. And dogs like these deserve nothing less. Mind your own business, I'll do what I want."

He had a surprisingly educated voice and spoke fluent Greek, but the troop commander intervened saying, "They are not our responsibility, my lady, these Jews do strange things; we'll have to let them get on with it," and with that Lydia, furious at the way the prisoners were being treated, turned away in disgust, with their cries ringing in her ears.

Lydia could not help but feel angry and sad to see such cruelty, and thought, *I never did like these people, all they ever seem to do is to hate, and they seem to make it a way of life.*

An hour later they had passed through the city gate and made their way up the hill to the palace. The troop commander went into the palace guardroom and a few minutes later came out with a soldier, who was told to take Lydia and her companions to the guest quarters in the citadel. Lydia remembered it well, and found her surroundings strangely comforting, even though the whole palace complex was filled with memories of that day when she had the awful dream that had started her on this quest.

Miriam, her Jewish maid from her previous home in Jerusalem, was still in the employ of the palace, but looked markedly older, and now had quite grey hair. She was told by the palace secretary, Marcus, to attend to the needs of lady Lydia and her companions whilst they were in residence, and to find out the length and details of her stay when they had settled into their quarters.

Lydia had met Marcus before, when her husband was procurator, he was a junior second secretary then, a Centurion by rank, but she had always found him to be a polite and respectful man – he was now a top grade of civil servant, just a little below the rank of tribune.

Marcus invited her into his office for a chat, and after the usual pleasantries, asked, "May I ask what your visit to Jerusalem is for, my lady? We have been having a lot of trouble of late with certain factions in the Jewish community being at each other's throats. This has been the cause of a breach of the peace on a number of occasions, and as ever I am aware of the security implications, particularly when we have guests. With all due respect, we do not usually have women guests – they are mainly senior army or government officers."

Lydia smiled. "Yes, I'm sure you must have certain misgivings, but I want to contact Nicodemus, a lawyer I am told. Do you know of him or how I can go about finding him?"

The secretary looked at her with raised eyebrows. "Nicodemus?" he questioned. "He is a very prominent member of the Sanhedrin, and a very controversial one at that. Yes he is in the capital; I can try and arrange for him to see you, but I would need to be assured of your safety."

Lydia gestured towards Alexander, who sat next to her. "My young friend here will look after me," she replied, "he's quite used to fighting! He's joining the army when we get back home, Procurator Marcellus encouraged him to do so at Tiberius before we left, and will sponsor him. But it would be better if you do not to tell Nicodemus who I am, only that I am in business in Rome."

"Quite so, my lady," he replied, "I think that would be wise!"

The meeting broke up with the secretary promising to do his best to arrange the meeting. "It won't be today," he said, "as it's the Jewish Sabbath. They do nothing on the Sabbath but make a lot of noise, so far as I can see." He laughed at his own joke. "It will probably be early next week."

That afternoon Lydia took Alexander into the main street of the city to show him the sights. She was given many hostile glances, but one look at her large companion – who had a useful-looking bejewelled sword, and a large dagger in his belt – warned off any one who might attempt to molest her. Although she could not understand the local language, the inflexions and intonation of what was being said and called out to her was enough to make her aware of the hostile intent of the bystanders. The Zealots were also a potential threat, not only to strangers, and Romans in particular, but even to their own people if they were inclined to mischief for political ends.

Two days later, the secretary came to find Lydia in her quarters. "I have contacted your lawyer at his office," he told her, "but he wants to know why you want to see him before he will grant you an interview."

"You did not tell him who I was, I trust?" she asked.

"No, I didn't even tell them your gender, that would have earned a refusal straightaway! But they do want to know why you want to see him," replied Marcus.

"Tell them I have come straight from the procurator in Tiberius," she laughed. "He'll have a surprise when he does meet me again, I met him at a reception we held for the Sanhedrin some years ago, and actually he did seem quite human. My husband thought he was one of the better ones. Let's see what he is like now! Anyway, see what you can do."

"You do realise, my lady, that he will not wish to be seen in the company of a member of the occupying powers. Things have changed a bit since you last met him."

"Yes I do realise that," she replied, "I have rarely met such suspicion in all my life," she said, shaking her head. "Everyone seems to be scared of their own skin."

However, the meeting was arranged to be held in the lawyer's private office which was attached to his villa on the outskirts of the city, away from prying eyes. Two days later Lydia and Alexander arrived – he on a mule and Lydia in a litter carried by two of the palace staff. It was mid-afternoon when Alexander knocked on the door of the office, which was opened at once by the lawyer's servant.

"Yes?" he enquired, looking over the young and rather tall Roman in surprise.

"Your master has an appointment to see my superior

from the palace," Alexander said in his most commanding voice.

"Yes, that's right," said the servant, somewhat overawed by this imposing young man.

"We'll come in then," said Alexander, beckoning to the bearers to bring Lydia in. Before the man had time to realise what was happening, Lydia and Alexander pushed him aside and went straight to the office door ahead of them. They knocked and walked in with the nonplussed servant gabbling away behind them that he didn't know who they were.

"Oh do be quiet, man," said Alexander as they entered the office to see the elderly lawyer sitting behind his desk filling in some papers.

He looked up and his jaw dropped with recognition coming almost at once. "My lady," he spluttered, "I didn't think it would be you. Please sit down, both of you," and he called for his servant to bring another chair.

Lydia laughed. "No, I'm sure you didn't. This is my young protégé Alexander, who I want to stay with me whilst we talk."

"It must be a few years since last we met at the palace," he remarked when he had recovered from his surprise . "If I may be so bold, time has been very good to you. Whatever do you want to see me about?"

They talked for a while about her husband and her problems since she had left Judea. He was sympathetic at the turn of events, but she did not tell him how her husband had died.

"How do you feel now about what happened here just before he was recalled to Rome?" he asked her. "There was quite a fuss."

"Your Sanhedrin twisted his arm," she replied firmly. "Pilate was a serving officer, but he was there to keep the peace, not judge theological matters, he lived and thought as a soldier, and anyone disturbing the peace was a threat to the state. But in the case we are so obviously referring to, he found the prisoner not guilty and said so, and would have let him go, had he not had his arm twisted. Of the details of that I am unaware, but would like to have known."

Nicodemus listened, looking very uncomfortable. "True, my lady, but he didn't have to have him crucified." Nicodemus' face was red with embarrassment.

Lydia repeated firmly, "He was a soldier, not a theologian, malcontents are executed daily by Rome if found guilty, but Rome did not – I repeat did not – find him guilty, you did. But what I want to know is why you and your friend asked for his body for burial, and in your friend's own tomb. Why? You told my husband he was a good man. Am I to infer from that remark that you considered him a better person than the members of the Sanhedrin?"

Nicodemus slumped down in his seat and put his head in his hands. Lydia felt sorry for him, he was an old man and now looked haggard. He then looked up and said, "I tried to save him but I didn't try hard enough, I was more concerned for my own position, I'm ashamed to admit."

They sat in silence for a moment. Alexander looked at Lydia in confusion, but she shook her head and gestured to him to be quiet. Nicodemus stood up and went to look out of the window in silence for a moment.

With his back to her he then quietly asked, "What is

it you want, my lady? It's not about that, is it? Joseph and I did our best after he was dead and your husband allowed us to have his body, but it disappeared from the tomb. Did you know that?" He turned and looked at her. "His followers said he came back to life, did you know that was what they claimed?"

"Yes," she said, "I do know that, and they were right – he did, and I think you know that too."

Nicodemus resumed his seat suddenly and looked at her in amazement. "How do you know?" he asked tremulously. "You couldn't!"

"Nicodemus," she began, "he still talks to me." She proceeded to tell him about the voice and all she had experienced these last few years. It took some time to tell him and afterwards he sat in silence for a while. He again turned and stood up to look out of the window, deep in thought.

"It's not finished, you know, it's only just starting," he said eventually. He turned back to her. "A lot of people believe he came back to life and the authorities are trying to suppress it. We had one young man, Stephen by name, hauled in front of us for blasphemy last week for his beliefs about that. I tried to speak for him but they wouldn't listen. They found him guilty and stoned him to death." He had tears running down his face as he went on, "Caiaphas, the High Priest, has got a new spymaster called Saul who is hauling the believers, men, women and children, before him and putting them in chains in prison and torturing them to death. As Stephen was being stoned, Saul stood there and held the clothes of the priests as they did it. He's like a wild beast, but worse than an animal. May God in his mercy forgive him."

"Is he a short bald headed man with a beard?" she asked Nicodemus, recognising his description.

"You've met him, my lady?" he asked.

"I'm afraid I had that misfortune," she replied. "He was herding prisoners in shackles along the road to prison as we came in last week, beating men, women and children with whips, a cruel man and I told him so, and received a mouthful of abuse for my pains!"

"He's off next week to the north on one of his witch hunts," Nicodemus said, "so perhaps we'll get peace for a while. But, my lady, I want to think about what you have told me and would be pleased to see you again. Incidentally, the maid at the palace is one of us. She had her husband taken by this Saul some time ago, so perhaps you would like to talk with her about the Master." This was the first time she had heard this title given to Jesus. "The Master was no respecter of any particular persons, you know. In his eyes, all were equal before their maker – no matter what their social or official position."

Lydia got up to go, then turned to Alexander. "This conversation is absolutely in confidence and must not be divulged to anybody without my permission," she said firmly. "The implications of what you have heard today are a major security concern, you do realise that?"

"Yes, my lady, I do realise that," he replied thoughtfully.

She held out her hand to Nicodemus, "Goodbye for the present and thank you, you have cleared up a lot of things for me that I was concerned about."

He stood up as he replied seriously. "Thank you, my lady, for coming to see me."

Lydia and Alexander turned to go. As she left the lawyer's office she thought with relief, *So he is still alive, my voice is not just an illusion or wishful thinking! I need to find out more.*

CHAPTER 9

On their return to the palace, Lydia was met by the secretary, who asked if she had had a satisfactory visit, and whether it had answered some of her questions.

"Oh yes, I found him very helpful, but he does look old. The last time we met he was quite sprightly," she replied.

"Yes indeed," he replied, "he is getting on a bit. As I said, he is a very controversial man and has upset a lot of his colleagues, and that must take its toll. He really is the cleverest one of a not very clever lot and can probably run rings around them in discussions – but then I am sure you remember what his colleagues are like. They haven't changed much over the years!" he laughed, sardonically.

Lydia smiled at his comments. "I've got to think about what he told me and will probably need to go back and see him again. He had a friend called Joseph, if I remember aright," she replied, "he was another lawyer, but I didn't ask about him. Is he still alive, do you know?"

"To the best of my knowledge he is, my lady. But he was pretty old when you were last here, though I've not heard of his death," he replied.

Lydia and Alexander relaxed in the atrium later that afternoon. They were on their own and Lydia asked him to check that their conversation would not be overheard as she began to discuss their visit to Nicodemus. Alexander was fully in Lydia's confidence by now, and was quite intrigued with the story as it had developed so far. He admired Lydia's method of eventually getting to the heart of the matter, it was as though she was peeling the skins off an onion one at a time, until she got to the core.

He had a lot of questions to ask, but she could not answer many. She had little knowledge of the man she was interested in, having never met him, and had only secondhand evidence that he had ever existed, apart from the stories told about him!

"Shall we ask Miriam?" he asked her. "She might be helpful and fill in some of the details as the lawyer said – you say she was here with you at the time?"

Miriam came into the room a few minutes later with some refreshing drinks.

"Ah, Miriam," said Lydia.

"Yes, Madame," replied Miriam in a dispirited way, "what can I do for you?"

"Miriam, I was sorry to learn that your husband has been arrested. What has he been charged with?" Lydia asked.

Miriam put down the tray of drinks and said guardedly, "Yes, Madame, that's true. He has been arrested, but if you will excuse me, I'd rather not talk about it."

"Well I do not wish to intrude into your affairs," Lydia persisted, "but I was talking to the lawyer Nicodemus yesterday..." she had not finished the sentence before Miriam burst into tears. "I'm sorry Miriam," continued Lydia contritely, "but I'm trying to piece together the events of that last week before I left with my husband. You do know that he is dead, do you not?"

Miriam wiped her tears. "Yes, Madame, I do know that, I'm very sorry, but that was a dreadful week and it is too dreadful to think about it, I'm sorry but I can't help you."

"All right, Miriam, you get on with your work," said Lydia sympathetically. "I'm sorry I've upset you. I won't ask you again."

As Miriam left the room, Alexander remarked, "We're not going to get far with her, she's not going to talk with us, what's the problem?"

"We are," smiled Lydia, "but we represent authority, doesn't matter which one, whether its theirs or ours, to her we represent the people who arrested her husband!"

Later that day, Marcus came to find them. "My lady," he said, "in conversation with the under secretary this morning, I asked him if he had heard anything recently of Nicodemus' friend Joseph, and he told me that he believed he still lived in the same house, but was now very frail and spent most of his time either sleeping or reading." He turned to Alexander, "If you would go and introduce yourself to him, I'm sure you could arrange for my lady to visit him."

Alexander looked at Lydia, who nodded her approval. "Yes I could do that if you tell me where to find him," he replied.

"You'll have to go with one of our security people as it is out of town some way. Take one of the mules, I'll give you a chit to get one from the stables and details of his address," the secretary said.

With Lydia's approval, Alexander went that afternoon. He was away only a short time and she greeted him on return with, "Well how did you get on?"

Alexander grinned ruefully. "Like all the rest, it's like getting blood out of a stone. No he won't speak to you, my lady, they're all so suspicious. What's the matter with them?"

"They are all very frightened people. Oh well, we'll have to try another tack, though it's understandable if, like Miriam, they think that by talking to the wrong people, they are going to get arrested by this spymaster of theirs. They're not going to talk to us, so I shall have to go back to Nicodemus and see what he thinks. We seemed to have gained his confidence, but I want to find out how and why this man Jesus has had such an impact. Is he the voice of my dreams, because I think he is!"

Alexander laughed. "You don't want to know much, do you, my lady!" he said.

"I'm going to find out," she said in a determined voice, "and with the secretary's permission, I'm going to talk to the legal officer and see if I can trawl through the court records and see what went on that day. My husband insisted that everything was recorded in detail – as he once remarked, 'If you keep accurate records of past happenings, you can set a precedent to obtain justice for today'. Wise words indeed, but I feel this is not a criminal case, and this so–called criminal is not stupid as most criminals are, in that they get caught! A point he once made to me when he judged a case in which a man was hung for theft, getting drunk on the wine in the house he was burgling. The householder found him asleep with his loot on the floor of the bedroom! Now that is stupid!"

Alexander laughed. "Serve the fool right too," he said.

"No, I think this is a case of good old-fashioned jealousy, greed, fear, and intolerance of another person's beliefs," she murmured.

Lydia spent the rest of the afternoon with the palace legal officer, trawling through the court records until she came to the case. It was all rather confusing. The prisoner had not initially been brought before the court, but had been judged and sentenced by the Jewish court. In their eyes he was guilty of blasphemy, which, according to the law of Moses – the code by which all their disputes were dealt with – demanded the death sentence. However, with the Roman occupation of the state, this facility had been removed from the Sanhedrin and they were not allowed to execute anybody without permission of the Roman authority.

So the prisoner was first examined by a senior public servant in the Sanhedrin, to whom he refused to talk. Eventually, he had ended up in front of her husband in a public trial outside the court and was found not guilty. There were no witnesses for his defence; it was stated that one Simon Peter, a Galilean fisherman who was a close accomplice of the prisoner, had denied any knowledge of him on arrest, and had escaped custody in the melee and could not be found.

However, the representatives of the High Priest pointed out that it was necessary for the prisoner to be executed because of his subversive behaviour. He was not only threatening the Jewish state by disturbing the peace as he had done on numerous occasions, he was also a threat to Rome, the occupying power, under whose wise government they lived safely! If the procurator would not comply with their request, it would appear that he was either sympathetic to, or in league with, those that would attempt to destabilise this peace attained under Roman rule. If that was so, they would need to petition the emperor himself to get justice done! Dreadful people! However, the procurator had eventually decided to release to them another detainee in his place eventually because of their continued plea and implied threat. He had allowed the High Priest to take the prisoner away for execution to keep the peace. The case was closed as the procurator ceremoniously washed his hands, declaring that he still found the prisoner not guilty.

Lydia closed the file. "That looked a mess," she said to the legal officer. "I now know the pressure my husband was put under, but he did still have the choice!"

She walked out of the archives and thought, *I did warn him, in fact begged him not to get involved. He didn't have to, the emperor would not have listened to that lot, so why did he get involved by letting them kill him?* The thought nagged at her for the rest of the day.

The next day, they went back to see Nicodemus. He greeted her politely, "My lady , I'm glad to see you, and I must tell you that I was ashamed to admit to my inability or possible reluctance to intervene in the case we talked about the other day. I have now given a lot of thought to this. I've tried in the past to put it out of my mind, but I must now follow it through to its logical conclusion. Therefore in the circumstances, I am forced to renounce my membership of the Sanhedrin and will publicly inform the house next week of the reasons for my resignation. In all conscience, if I as a lawyer cannot do my utmost to see that justice is done, what am I doing at the bar?"

Lydia looked at this worried elderly man and felt remorse that she had brought matters to such a pitch, but now, having seen the transcript , there could be no going back. She told him about the transcript of the trial she had read yesterday and how all involved, including herself, had not tried hard enough either. She felt all were to blame, all had reasons for their actions of course, but they were mainly selfish ones. Nobody came out of the affair with any credit and she observed that he, Nicodemus, was only guilty in that he too hadn't tried hard enough. She could now see that everyone had committed misdemeanors of the most heinous nature, including her husband.

Nicodemus thought for a moment and then said quietly, "No, my lady, sins of omission are just as bad as those of commission. I must do this now. I haven't got many years left, and need to meet my maker with a clear conscience."

"You will, I am sure, do what is right, but this is a very complex matter and I must get to the bottom of it. I still don't know what happened since his death. Who, by the way, is Simon Peter. Is he still involved?"

Nicodemus sighed. "Yes, he's the present leader with James, who was the Master's brother. They go from safe house to safe house to avoid arrest. If Saul caught them, I dread to think how he would treat them. Fortunately, there are many safe houses. The movement has really gained many followers, but that's what persecution does."

She told him about Joseph. "He is my dearest friend," he said. "He had nothing to do with any of this, but it was his tomb he offered to me to bury the Master in. I'll tell him about you the next time I see him, but that will depend upon my situation when I resign from the Sanhedrin."

Lydia and Alexander returned to the palace that evening. As they came in past the guardroom, Lydia said to Alexander, "We don't seem to be able to get anywhere, do we? Or at least not far enough to make any great sense of all this. But if this Saul is going away for a time, the locals might relax a bit and talk to us. However, I feel that our only local contact, Miriam, may well change her mind and let slip a few facts that we can work on. We'll have to lay low for a few days and see what happens. I'm only interested in getting to the truth of the matter. I wish none of this movement any harm. I just want the truth. I can recall my husband talking once in his rather cynical way about the truth 'What is truth?' It depends, he said, upon where you stand!"

Alexander looked puzzled; his intellectual skills were not as well honed as those of Lydia, who had spent many lonely hours in the palace reading the great philosophers, both ancient and modern. "I'm not sure what you mean, my lady," he said, "a thing is either true or it is false."

"Not so," replied Lydia. "What is true to one man is false to another, it depends upon his ethics. After all, a habitual burglar will see nothing wrong with robbing the rich if he thinks it unfair that they have more than him. However, he would not like to rob the poor if his ethics demanded that the poor were more worthy than the rich, because it would be wrong for the rich man to get money at the expense of the poor, do you follow me? But the rich man thinks, according to his ethics, that the only way to earn money is to work hard, no matter how he gets it – even if he has to oppress the poor to do it!"

"I see what you mean, but if he used the money, even if he earned it honestly, to oppress the poor, that would be wrong."

Lydia laughed, "You're getting there," she said, "but to the matter in hand; we'd better lay low for the time being. The palace won't mind us staying here, it gives them something different to do."

Two days later, Miriam asked Lydia if she could talk to her alone and in private. Lydia was happy to do this. In her eyes, Miriam was a free woman, and although a member of the indigenous population, she was a paid employee of the Roman administration, so was more on a level with Lydia than the slaves who worked in the kitchen and did all the dirty work.

In Roman society you were either a slave or free. Free meant you were born free, that is, not into slavery, but slaves could be given their freedom after a period of time or as a gesture from their masters. They were then designated freed men, and their offspring were therefore born free. She had discovered that the spymaster Saul was free, but he had been born to freedmen, so had the classification of free. It was a great honour to be freed; the person could then benefit from all the privileges of the state and had access to all the good things of the Empire. This was unlike the slave, who was the property of a master who could do what he wanted with him – and even lawfully kill him if he wanted to, and felt he had justification to do so.

So, Lydia invited Miriam to come and sit next to her.

She had told Alexander not to come in as she knew that Miriam would not relax in the presence of a man.

"Miriam, I do understand your predicament. Alexander is rather an imposing young man, but he is in my confidence and will not divulge anything I tell him of our conversation, if I do tell him anything. We are both puzzled about what is going on and want to get to the bottom of this because, as you know, my husband was involved and what happened grieved me greatly."

Lydia smiled and touched Miriam's arm. "But," she continued, "I am not like the average member of my clan. I was brought up by very loving parents; my father always had respect for his fellow men, whether slave or free. He used to say, 'Why abuse your staff? They are the ones who keep you in the lifestyle to which you are accustomed and earn your money for you.' I subscribe to those ethics, so what is it you want to tell me?"

Miriam looked at Lydia and smiled. "Thank you, Madame," she said quietly, "I do know what you are like and have always felt comfortable in your presence, but I'm afraid I never did in the company of your husband or his colleagues. However, you wanted to know about my husband's arrest. Well he was with a number of his friends, who were all followers of 'The Way', as we call it, when the meeting was broken up by the Temple police. How they found them I don't know, but there must have been an informer somewhere. He is to be released next week, I have been told, as nobody could testify against them because they were only studying the Torah. It is no offence, children have to learn great chunks of it at school after all, but the police claimed it was suspicious as it is not usually studied otherwise, except by the rabbis in the synagogue. That was all, but poor Aaron was beaten up by them and has got a black eye I am told."

"What exactly is the Torah?" asked Lydia. "It's not subversive, is it?"

"No, Madame, it's the code we Jews live by, the law as revealed to Moses."

"Revealed?" questioned Lydia.

"Yes," replied Miriam. "Centuries ago, when the Jews escaped from Egypt, God called their leader Moses and told him what they must do to establish the state of Israel. This Torah, where it is all written down, contains many laws and instructions that we think are redundant now, but were essential in those early days to provide direction for the large number of people travelling through desert lands to what is now Israel. These rules and laws made sure that people would survive, giving instructions on food, health, clothing , personal behaviour, and so on. It laid down laws concerning punishment for anyone that threatened the tribes as they journeyed, and so ensured the stability of the state, and family matters."

"That sounds a good book," remarked Lydia. "And you use it today?"

"Yes, Madame, but the powerful leaders of today insist that all the rules are to be obeyed implicitly, and insist that all Jews obey them on pain of punishment or even death, but the powerful people do not themselves obey them. The instructions include giving to the poor, care and treatment of the sick, and showing mercy when necessary. If they were to obey them, they would not be able to live the rich and selfish lives they do. They would not like to treat others as themselves or give up their privileged lives, so they wield their power by making sure that others obey the laws, when they do not."

"Oh dear, the old problem of clever people who can handle words and make them say whatever they want them to mean," Lydia sighed, "particularly if they can benefit from them!"

"Yes, that's the problem we have here, but they are not really very clever. They may be well educated, but they are devious and obstinate. The Master really upset them, because he told them that they obeyed the letter of the law and not the spirit, and said that in reality they did neither," said Miriam. "So they got rid of him!"

"But he was one of their own! You would have expected a little sympathy from them for another point of view, not the extreme hatred that was shown," observed Lydia.

"It put them in a difficult position, Madame. They couldn't continue their evil ways if they were to use the law correctly, but then abuse the poor, sick and less advantaged than themselves." explained Miriam.

"Ah, I see, the old problem, so what's new?" Lydia said, sardonically.

Miriam continued, "They claim, of course, that their motivation comes from God, but the Master said they were liars, as he is the son of God, and he told the so in no uncertain terms!"

"He said what?" Lydia continued with raised eyebrows "That he is the son of God? But that's unbelievable. Which god? There are many gods."

"We believe there is only one God, who made the world and all within it. The Master is his son, and his father sent him to earth to sort out these greedy people. He is our long promised Messiah. That's what he said, and we believe him; it was foretold in the scriptures after all. So we believers are now the enemy of the rich and powerful, but more and more people are coming to believe in him, and are joining us because we know he holds the truth that makes our lives better. He allows us to exercise our choice; we are not being fixed in a selfish ideology that stops us thinking. Others claim they are right, but we think that the only man who was right was crucified and then rose again."

"Thank you Miriam," said Lydia, shaking her head in wonderment, "I shall have to go and think about this and explain it to Alexander. Yes, so it is true then. He did rise from the dead, or at least his ideas have!"

"I will, if I may, take you to see a man who was with him after his resurrection," Miriam said hesitantly, "and he will confirm all I have told you. He is now our leader, he's called Cephas. Will you come, Madame?"

"Oh yes," replied Lydia, "I will. How could I refuse?"

Lydia later repeated to Alexander the gist of the conversation she had had with Miriam that evening. Alexander listened carefully, before commenting, "But just because they believe all that, doesn't mean it's true."

"No," she replied, smiling, "but because something is true, you don't have to believe it either! Remember what we talked about yesterday, that truth can be determined by the position you hold. As you say, when you believe does not mean it is true – but conversely, simply because it is true, doesn't mean you have to believe it!"

"Well, do you believe it?" he asked her.

"I'm not sure, but I'd like to do as Miriam suggests and go and see this Cephas. Please don't repeat that name to anyone – security again, I'm afraid," she replied. "I would like to meet him and hear what he has to say as he claims to have been with the Master after his resurrection."

"Do you want me to come with you?" he asked.

"No, I'll be safer with Miriam, she knows everyone, and has her own friends to protect her."

A couple of days later, Miriam told Lydia that she would be going to see Cephas that evening, and if she would like to come with her she should be prepared to wear local dress. "You'll be safer with me than if you are wearing Roman clothing," she told her.

Miriam and Lydia, wearing appropriate dress, arrived at a large house just as it was getting dark. The house had a commodious upper room. There were guards on the door checking everyone in; they looked suspiciously at Lydia, but Miriam assured them that she was a friend of hers from the country who did not speak Aramaic, so she would interpret for her. They were ushered into a room containing quite a large crowd of people sitting and talking to each other, both men and women, and were offered wine and biscuits. Miriam introduced Lydia to a Greek-speaking friend of hers who welcomed Lydia with a kiss. This surprised Lydia, as she was unused to kissing in public, which to her was a very intimate thing to do, but she wanted to fit in with the people Miriam had told her about so took it in her stride.

Suddenly, a tall bearded man with a weather-beaten face stood up and called for silence. He welcomed them all in the name of the Master and said he and wanted to talk tonight about their treatment of strangers. Miriam whispered to Lydia that this was Cephas. He had quite a compelling personality and began to talk about a brush the Master had had with some lawyers who were questioning him as to why he said we must treat all our neighbours as we would like to be treated ourselves. They wanted to know who he defined as his neighbour. Miriam tried to keep up interpreting for Lydia, who understoood mosr of what was said but hoped to talk to the man later.

Cephas went on telling the story, "A man was travelling home down the road to Jericho – do know it?" he asked. His audience nodded. "Well he got mugged," he said.

"Not unusual," said a member of the meeting, laughing. "I wouldn't want to go down there unless I was escorted by cavalry!"

Cephas nodded in agreement. "He'd lost all his clothing and his mule, and was badly beaten up. As he lay there, along came three men. 'Thank God,' he said 'they will help me.' The first man, who was a Levite, came over and looked at him and turned away in disgust. *What a nasty untidy mess*, thought the Levite. *Why was the fool walking along here without a guard? It serves him right. He's only a working man, I'm not descending to his level. I'm wanted soon at the Temple for the evening sacrifice; that's more important than this creature,* and he walked on.

"The second man was a rabbi. He took one look at the blood, and said, 'I can't touch him. Leviticus, in the law, says you must not touch blood, only the blood of sacrifices. If I did I'd be unclean. How can I preach to my congregation if I am unclean? God would never forgive me.' So there we have two men who should have known better: one wouldn't help and the other couldn't help.

"But the third man was a Samaritan – a deviant, they teach us, a man we don't talk to if we are a proper Jew. Well he stopped and said to him, 'Oh dear, you poor chap,' and promptly sorted out his wounds. He then put him on his donkey, took him to an inn and paid his keep for three days.

"So the Master asked the lawyers, who was a neighbour to the man? Was it the Levite who wouldn't help, because the poor wounded chap was socially beneath him; the priest who couldn't help because the law said he mustn't touch blood apart from sacrifices; or the Samaritan, who helped the man, who through no fault of his own couldn't help himself?

"The lawyers had to admit it was the horrible old Samaritan – the man they wouldn't give house room to – and that didn't go down well with them. The Master was cleverer than all the clever people, which is why they hated him. So don't forget: everybody is our neighbour! Whether Samaritans or Romans, all are God's children, made by him and for him." There was silence in the room for a few moments and a few shuffled their feet: these were strong words.

Cephas continued, "But you are free to help, you've got a brain and you have a choice. Others, because of their bigoted beliefs, have not, and that's not living! The Master promised us a better life, free from the fear of our enemies. They'll try and stop you, but in the end will not beat God at his own game. He promised us life and that we might have it more abundantly." And with that he sat down to grunts of approval and a few tears from the women present.

Lydia had listened to this man carefully as Miriam interpreted for her. *This is a wise man,* she thought, *obviously not well educated or out of the top drawer, but with words worth listening to!*

Before they left the room, Miriam introduced her to Cephas and told him that Lydia knew Zacheus in Tiberius. A grin spread over his face, and in hesitant Greek he said, "Give him my love and the Master's blessing, and I'll hope to see him soon."

Lydia went back to the palace very impressed with the meeting and Cephas.

The next morning, the palace security officer came to find Lydia. "My lady," he began in an embarrassed voice, "I understand that last night you went to see some undesirables. I'm afraid you were seen by the Temple police and I have been advised that you should stay within the palace complex until you return to Tiberius."

Lydia was shocked. "What about Miriam?" she asked.

"They apparently know all about her, and are keeping an eye on her. If you stay in Jerusalem and, as they put it, interfere in the internal affairs of their administration, they will not be able to guarantee her safety. So I'm afraid that in order to keep the somewhat fragile peace that we enjoy, you will have to return to Tiberius. I have recommended to the palace secretary, who will arrange your journey back with the despatches column, and that you go tomorrow at first light."

Lydia looked shocked and was speechless for a moment, so the security officer continued. "In the meantime I have just learnt that a leading lawyer, one Nicodemus, was found dead in his garden this morning, stabbed through the heart. Apparently he had just retired from the Sanhedrin on health grounds. The Temple Police understand you went to visit him recently and want to know why, as there will have to be a murder enquiry . The High Priest has called for three days of mourning for this, I quote, 'most beloved and witty man who gave his all to the Temple and who will be greatly missed'. You'll have to go I'm afraid, my lady."

Lydia looked at the officer. "I've stirred up a lot of trouble since I've been here, but for them to kill that dear, kindly old man…a man as honest as the day is long – words fail me." She wiped the tears from her eyes .

"I'm afraid that is how frightened people in government work, my lady. These Jewish politicians are jealous and will get up to any trick in the book to maintain the power they have, but just let them try it on with a Roman citizen and I can assure you, they would live to regret it, whoever and however high in the hierarchy they are – the bigger they are, the harder they fall!"

"What a despicable lot they are!" she said, her voice breaking. "The man who started all this was killed by them three to four years ago! As with this case, putting pressure on others to justify your behaviour is appalling; It's tantamount to blackmail. It's exactly what they did to my poor husband! Yes, it is blackmail! Now I know how my husband must have felt."

CHAPTER 10

The long journey to Tiberius began at first light. There was bad weather on the way and it was already cold with a smattering of rain as they cantered out of the city gate into the dull grey countryside. A thick fog slowed them down to start with, but the road, built by the Roman Army engineers, was well defined, and as the fog began to clear, they clattered along at a good speed. The troop commander of the escort wanted to keep up a good pace and take no more than two days to cover the distance. It was not a comfortable journey, but Lydia was glad to leave the confines of the city, although she was sad at having to leave behind those friendly souls who had accepted her and Alexander. She really felt they were at risk of arrest having been seen in her company, and she knew the lengths the authorities could go to if suspicious of her motives.

The troop commander informed her that ahead was a column of Jewish police, also mounted on horseback, who were taking the spymaster Saul to his next appointment in the north. She was glad to hear this, hoping it would give a little peace to those of 'The Way' back in the capital, now this dreadful man was out of the city and its surrounding villages.

Lydia still felt outraged at how the visit had turned out, with both her and Alexander being virtually hounded out of the capital. However, she was glad to have met such wonderful people as Nicodemus and

Miriam again. Alexander, with little knowledge of the working of the politician's minds, assumed their treatment was normal, but Lydia was unable to express to him the utter disgust she felt at the way the Jewish politicians functioned. It was only later, when she was back in Rome, that she came to understand how religion and politics were one and the same thing in Judea.

Last night after she had dozed off in bed, the voice had come to her again. "Lydia, there will be many more troubles ahead for you, but you will gain your reward."

Once again she was unaware of the meaning, but each time the voice spoke, there was always something strangely comforting in the words. She pondered on this as they rode along, until they arrived tired and saddle – sore at the rest house to stay the night. The weather had broken; it was now raining heavily and they were glad to get out of the cold and wet into the comparative warmth of the building. The winter had come early, and the staff were not fully prepared for the cold weather, but after a rudimentary hot meal they went to bed happy that tomorrow would see them at journey's end.

Leaving early the next morning for the last few miles to Tiberius, it was with relief that they breasted the last hill on the road. There below was the lake again whose water was rough and grey with large waves breaking over the quayside. Eventually they clattered into the palace, past the guardroom with the gate guard at attention saluting the troop commander as they passed, and arrived at last at the guest quarters of the palace to a warm, dry welcome. Julia came out to meet Lydia – she had wanted to accompany Lydia to the capital, but when told of their experiences was glad that she had not.

However, all had changed in the two months they had been away: Marcellus, who she knew well, had been replaced as procurator on promotion by Marullus. Marcellus had left Lydia a note advising her not to talk to the new procurator about her journey's quest as he was a hardliner and averse to anything to do with religion, and that of the Jews in particular. He wished her well and wrote that when she returned to Rome after winter he would, if he might, call upon her and hear her story.

Lydia met the new procurator that evening and told him that she would be returning to Rome at the earliest opportunity, which would in all probability be in some three months' time on the first sailing possible from Caesarea. Marullus was helpful and advised her that she would be welcome to stay until then, but Alexander would also have to go with her as he had plans for the province that did not include the presence of a rich civilian. Not that Alexander had expressed any wish to stay in the province, however, as he wanted to get back and join the army.

The following morning dawned bright and clear. The storm had blown itself out, and the scene by the lake was peaceful again with the fishing boats apparently getting ready to sail again that evening. Lydia had spent the morning with Alexander comparing notes about the visit, and although Alexander was sceptical about the events and the implications of what he had observed, he had some sympathy towards the aspirations of those he had met.

Later that morning he wandered down to the quayside, enjoying the sunshine and the walk. He saw

Zacheus' office on the quay and on impulse went in. The clerk told him that Zacheus was not in and had gone to see his friend Job in the town, however he would soon be back if Alexander would care to wait on the seat outside the office.

So, Alexander sat on the quayside and enjoyed the sun and mild breeze. It was so quiet after the hurly-burly and bustle of the city, and as he relaxed he watched the fishermen preparing their boats under the direction of a well–dressed smiling man who the fishermen referred to as Reuben. Alexander suddenly recalled that this was the name of the man who had turned his business over to his workers, so when Reuben finished his supervision and stood up to leave, he went up to him. Reuben looked at him in surprise as he was not used to young Roman men, particularly well–off ones, approaching him.

"Good morning," Alexander began, "are you the Reuben that Zacheus spoke of, who is the owner of the fishing fleet?"

"Indeed I am," he replied pleasantly. "Can I help you?"

Alexander smiled. "I've heard of your philanthropy and was impressed with the idea behind what you have done for your workers. Can I talk to you?"

Reuben invited him to come to the local tavern and together they sat outside with a jug of wine between them. "So you know Zacheus?" began Reuben.

"Yes, I am the guardian and companion of lady Lydia from Rome. She's on a fact-finding tour and we have just returned from Jerusalem," he told him. "We spoke to Zacheus just before we left two months ago."

"Oh yes, that's right, I remember now. How is she? Did you enjoy the trip?"

"You'd better ask her yourself," he replied with a rueful grin. "We're on the next ship back to Rome in the new year. It was not a very comfortable exercise, but we did get a lot of information and had some excitement as well. I'd rather let her tell you what happened though. Would you be prepared to meet her? She admires what you've done with your company, and is a businesswoman with a lot of influence in Rome."

"I'd be pleased to," he replied warily, "though you'd better talk to Zacheus about it, he's my father-in-law by the way, but in the meantime I must go, I've got another appointment at the boatyard at midday." He glanced up at the sun, "it's nearly that now, but I'm sure we'll meet again soon for a longer chat, so good day to you." And after shaking Alexander's hand, he mounted his donkey and went . *They all seem to shy away,* Alexander thought, *what's the problem?*

Alexander went back to his seat on the quay and resumed his relaxing observation of the busy boating scene, when suddenly he was hailed by name and saw the little taxman standing by the door of his office. Zacheus beckoned him over, shook hands, and Alexander told him how he had just met Reuben and had a few words with him. He told Zacheus that Reuben had agreed to meet Lydia some time and asked if Zacheus would be able to arrange a meeting for them all. Zacheus agreed to this and the arrangement was made for them to meet the following morning to finalise a time and date.

Returning to the palace, Alexander went to find Lydia, who was in the library reading. She looked up at him and smiled. "You've something to tell me," she observed.

"How do you know that, my lady?" he replied grinning. "But yes, I've just met Zacheus again, and also Reuben, the chap who organised the business for his workers."

"Oh that's marvelous," she replied, obviously very pleased. "And what was the outcome of your meeting?"

"I'm to meet him again at his office tomorrow to fix the time and place."

"Were they hesitant this time? she asked.

"Not quite so much as at our previous meeting. They seem to be two very open people and I think they know now that we mean them no harm. Do I go ahead?"

"Yes indeed," she replied.

The next day it was all arranged, and one evening they all gathered in Reuben's villa, with Reuben's pretty wife Miriam, to have a meal. The talk to start with was about family matters and Reuben's baby son Benjamin in particular. Miriam's companion Rosa popped in and out making sure they had enough to eat, and when the subject of babies had been exhausted, to the great relief of Alexander, the conversation turned to national matters. The news had just arrived that Agrippa had just been appointed king of all Palestine – he was a Jew but a Romanised one, and they could see that the few Jews in this mainly Roman part of the state would now be given privileges that had been denied to them before. *Perhaps*, thought Lydia, *this is what Marullus meant when he spoke of changes. The Jews up to now have had to keep their heads down, I wonder what this will do to the Pax Romana.*

But Lydia was more interested in how and why Reuben had done what he had done for his workers. When he said it was because this is what the Master would have wanted, Lydia was all ears. "How did you come under the influence of his teachings?" she asked him.

Reuben looked at her, his eyes smiling. "I met him after he rose from the dead," he said firmly, obviously expecting to see scorn or even bewilderment in her face. "It changed my life forever, and that of my father–in–law here." He gestured to Zacheus. "The Master was the man who cured my paralysis when I was a youngster. At the time I had no idea who he was. You never met him of course, but he was a wonderful man!"

Lydia sighed. "Would that I had, but he does talk to me." She then went on to tell him her story. "And so there it is," she said, and then told him about her realisation of what the politicians had done to her husband, and the news of poor Nicodemus.

There was a shocked hush. Reuben said in a quiet voice, "Nobody said it was going to be easy, and it's not." They sat and grieved in silence for their well-loved friend.

As Alexander and she left just before midnight, she gave the message from Cephas to Zacheus. He thanked her sadly, hoping Cephas would be safe in Jerusalem for the time being, and that he would come and see him in the near future if he could get away.

"Have you known him long?" Lydia asked.

He smiled. "Well his home is here," he replied. "He worked the lake with Reuben's mentor in the early days, when he was Simon Peter. It was the Master who called him Cephas – 'the rock' – later."

"Well that clears that up then, I did wonder," she said, and then told him of Saul's absence as he journeyed north. "Well, thank God for that, that should give them all some respite," he said heavily.

Lydia and Alexander were now marooned in Tiberius for the winter. They could have travelled overland to Rome, but it would have taken three months or more, and the journey would have been both uncomfortable and fraught with danger, and although the writ of Rome ran in each country between Judea and the capital, there were many dissidents and bandit gangs that no army, however large, would find possible to police .

It was annoying to Lydia that, having been chased out of Jerusalem by the Sanhedrin there was little to do in Tiberius to keep her active mind occupied. She had visited Miriam, Reuben's wife, on a number of occasions, and had had a pleasant time with her and her little son. However, though Miriam was very accepting of Lydia, culturally they were miles apart – Lydia was steeped in the classic philosophical culture of Greece and Rome, and Miriam under the unquestioning sway of the Torah, which she knew by heart and had learned by rote.

Lydia asked her if she could talk to her about the Torah, about why she accepted the idea that the Master was the son of God, and how she squared this with the teaching of the Torah, which Lydia understood was a system of law laid down in tablets of stone and not open to interpretation. Unfortunately it was difficult to engage at an intellectual level; emotionally there was no problem, but when Lydia asked about Miriam's understanding of the Torah and the basis of its origins, all she received was 'It was so from the beginning', and she could get no further. It was not that Miriam was reluctant to talk to her, but she had no knowledge, and had never been asked to think about it or its origins, or question any of it in a critical way.

To Lydia, there was something in the beliefs of the Master that she couldn't get her teeth into. Yes, his teaching made his adherents behave in a very civilised and kindly way, in a society which was harsh and often cruel in its judgments and actions to those unable to help themselves – the poor and oppressed, the sick and downtrodden. But what was it that made those who heard and received his message be so accepting of it, to the point where some would suffer ignominy and even death when convinced of its rightness?

In Jerusalem the followers of 'The Way' were convinced that he was the actual son of their God, and that he was the promised Messiah, or 'the one who was to come.' They believed that when he returned, as he said he would, all would live in peace and tranquillity. However, the traditionalists did not think so and were convinced that instead, when the Messiah came, he would be a warrior king who by force of arms would wrest the nation from the occupying enemy, Rome, and restore the nation to its greatness as a world power to whom every knee would bow in subjection.

So, how did this Jesus fit in? This man who went around doing good and healing the sick, who talked about loving one's neighbour, and the reign of justice and peace. How could he be this Messiah? She knew what she preferred, but in politics you didn't get your preferences, and certainly not in Rome. You got what the already powerful wanted, and you either accepted it or ran the risk of death or possible imprisonment.

But the spectral being that she had first seen the day before he was crucified was not an illusion. It was too vivid and the messages she received always seemed to fit the equation, at least up to now. So she sat and puzzled over it, and sometimes wondered why she was so fixed on the idea, but she couldn't just leave it alone. She was convinced for some reason that there was something there, and that she would hopefully one day have the answer.

The days passed slowly until spring eventually arrived, and to her great relief she could travel to Caesarea with Alexander and Julia, and board the ship home. But after obtaining passage on a ship destined for Rome, they put in to Corinth in the north to fill up with supplies and water, and were delayed for a further week by adverse wind and storms.

On the first evening of their arrival in Corinth, Alexander decided to wander away from the ship into the town to stretch his legs. On strolling down the main street, he heard laughter and singing from a house, and as he came up to it the doorman called to him, "Come inside and experience the love of God!"

Out of curiosity, Alexander followed the man into a room where there were a number of people who were singing. They were sitting around a table, both men and women together, drinking wine and eating small chunks of bread. The leader of the group, who sat at the head of the table, called to him, "Welcome, my friend! Come and share in the body and blood of the Lord with us Christians."

Alexander looked at him askance and asked, "Who are you, are you followers of Mithras?"

"No," replied the man with a smile. "We commemorate the death of the Christos, who was crucified in Jerusalem some years ago, and we remember his death every time we eat or drink as he told us to."

Alexander began to feel uncomfortable, so made his excuses and left rapidly. After having a brief conversation with the doorman of the house, he later told Lydia about his experience.

"Who were they?" she asked. "Are they talking about the same person we heard about in Jerusalem, the Master they called him? But this term Christian, what does it mean?"

"Apparently, accordingly to the doorman, the word Christos means 'the one who is to come', or the one the Jews called the Messiah. I assume it's the same thing," replied Alexander.

Lydia scratched her head. "This is all getting too much. Why should Greeks be doing this? We are miles away from Jerusalem, and these people are not Jews." She sighed. "But I doubt if there is anybody in Rome who can enlighten me! Christians? Followers of the Christos presumably."

But she was wrong; unbeknown to her, the tyrant Saul, following an incident on one of his many witch hunts, had also heard a voice, but in broad daylight, so compelling that it brought him to his knees and caused him to change sides. He was now called Paul, and was beginning to explain the life and death of the Master, and how it would affect anyone who believed in him, if only they would listen. And now, the message of peace and love was gaining ground, and would one day, possibly in Lydia's lifetime, even get as far as the imperial capital!

CHAPTER 11

The rest of the journey home passed slowly, as a strong westerly wind delayed their passage. It was not until the ship rounded the toe of Italy and they came under the lee of Sicily that the wind moderated and they were able to complete the voyage, which was taking two weeks longer than expected.

Lydia was impatient to get home to see how the spring crop-planting was progressing on her farms and to hear all the news. She had learned from the ship's master that Emperor Caligua had fallen out with both the senate and the army because of his extraordinary demands. It was rumoured that he too would suffer the fate of so many of his predecessors who had taken their eyes off the ball and allowed self-indulgence to take over from prudence. Anyone who threatened the stability of the state did not last long!

Alexander was impatient for other reasons. He'd already made up his mind that he would join the Praetorian Guard: he had all the right qualifications, a rich background, a classical education; he was a well built, tall, intelligent, and good-looking young man who carried himself well; and was convinced in his own mind that he would make a good officer in that prestigious regiment. He also knew from his recent experiences of rubbing shoulders with the senior officers in Judea, and with Marcellus the Procurator in particular, that he now had influential friends at court who would speak for him. He therefore wanted to start the process of enlistment as soon as possible.

Julia was just glad to be back on familiar ground, away from all the foreigners; it was not that she had met many of the natives of Judea, but the ones she had seen, and the poverty and disease she had witnessed, made them appear to her a scruffy and undisciplined lot that were best avoided.

It was evening on the last day of the voyage as they came into the bay of Ostia. The galley had to be warped to the jetty before tying up, and being first off the ship, Alexander went to find transport to carry them all to Lydia's estate. He managed to find and hire a suitable conveyance which was big enough for all three of them and their baggage, but it was nighttime before they were under way. Eventually they arrived at Lydia's villa and were met by her majordomo, Cassius, on the portico. He was not expecting her to arrive so late in the day, but Alexander had had the foresight to send a fast courier ahead to tell Cassius of their arrival at the port. Like the excellent servant he was, he had everything ready for them, and a light meal prepared for serving as soon as they had settled in.

"How nice to see you back safely," Cassius said. "I trust you had a safe and comfortable journey, my lady."

"Thank you, Cassius, as comfortable as any journey is," she laughed. "I don't suppose journeys are supposed to be comfortable, but some are better than others, and this fell into the latter category."

Lydia went to her bedroom and unpacked with the help of Julia, whilst Alexander settled himself down in the atrium and before dozing off remarking to Cassius, "Nice to sit on something solid that is not going up and down!"

"Quite so, sir," replied Cassius with a smile.

After they had eaten their evening meal, they all sat together in a companionable group and discussed the happenings of the last few months in Judea.

Alexander was not overenthusiastic about it all; he declared he was a man of action and to worry and argue about words, definitions and beliefs was not for him. However, Lydia pointed out that her upbringing in the classics and philosophy made it necessary for her to examine words, nuances and beliefs in others and she found it absolutely fascinating. This business of this Gallilean preacher had intrigued her, as had the juxtaposition of ideas: on one hand he was a compassionate teacher and healer, but on the other was an outspoken critic of the men he was so vehemently opposed to – and she found this disturbing in the extreme. She knew who she preferred, but contemplated that though the world may have changed a lot since the beginning of time, people – of whatever time, race or culture – had not .

In bed that night Lydia was again woken by the voice: "Keep seeking and you will find me!" On awakening she pondered these words. This spectre – or was it the Gallilean? – was making it difficult, giving her snippets of information but never enough. However, she was getting together quite a body of knowledge, and found that she could refer back to the voice quite easily. It seemed to have burnt a place into her memory, and she could remember every word he had said, but she felt that it slipped away from her just as she was beginning to know something.

Over the next few days, after Alexander had left for his home, Lydia spent time visiting all her farms and had long discussions with her managers and foremen. Gratius arrived unexpectedly one day looking rather pleased with himself, as though he had something important to talk to Lydia about.

"How lovely to have you back safe and well, Lydia," he began. "It's been a long haul; are you as well as you look?"

She laughed. "Brimming over with health, thank you," she replied, "and you?"

"Yes I'm very well," he replied, "and have some news for you. Caligula has been assassinated and Claudius has been appointed in his place."

"Who in heaven's name is Claudius, and how did all this come about?" she asked him, relieved that the threat had been lifted. "Is he going to be trouble?" she asked.

Gratius laughed. "No, the army got rid of Caligula. Claudius is their man – don't want anything upsetting the army, do we?"

Lydia replied hopefully, "So we should have peace and stability now. The Senate is always on about stability. They believe a stable society is the only way to get prosperity I believe, and I'm sure they're right. Aren't you?"

"True," replied Gratius, "but they had a bit of a tussle to start with as the Senate didn't want him, he's not a very martial figure. He's got a limp and a speech defect and is cross–eyed, you're never sure if he's looking at you or at somebody behind you! It is said the Praetorian Guard assassinated Caligula and afterwards when they found old Claudius hiding in the palace away from all the fuss, they dragged him out and made him Emperor, saying that he couldn't be worse than the last one, so he'll have to do! So, Claudius it is."

Lydia laughed. "If it wasn't so serious it would be funny, but really! It is a hard life being an emperor, but they do ask for trouble and seem to get it. Old Tiberius was the wisest, he just kept out of the way on his island and no one saw him."

Lydia had a sudden thought. "Was Centurion Augustus involved in the assassination?" she asked.

Gratius smiled. "Nobody was talking about personalities," he replied, "but by what you told me of him, it doesn't sound his style. Mind you, there are some real hard men in the guards, and they never take prisoners you know. Anyway, enough of that, how was your trip to Judea?"

Lydia looked down at her hands, then sighed. "Rather inconclusive I'd say, as I didn't find out a lot of what I went for. Something is missing and I don't think I'm going to find out until I get more information about the background of my quest. I need to talk to someone who can tell me what this Torah of the Jews says, and then I'm sure I will get more clues."

"Didn't you talk to any Jews in Judea about it?" asked Gratius.

"No, they won't talk to a Roman. They just shut up like a clam shell. I think they despise us as much as they think we despise them. They all know the words, having learnt them in childhood by rote, but haven't any understanding of their true meaning, having never been allowed to question them," replied Lydia.

"I know a Jew; he's a business associate of mine called Adonijah, and he would talk to you, he's a bright fellow. I'll have a word with him if you want," replied Gratius. "But to get to more important matters, are the farms doing well? We need to be looking to the future really." Gratius said thoughtfully, "So long as the grain ships can get through in time this year we will be alright, but the farming community ought to start looking ahead a bit more. We've wasted our surpluses up to now and need to conserve them to avoid shortages in future and build more granaries. Don't forget, we keep conquering more countries and that brings home thousands of slaves, which are all extra mouths to feed. If we had a shortage of food, the plebs would rise up and we would be in trouble."

Lydia looked at him. "Do you think we are likely to be in that sort of situation?" she asked seriously.

"We've cleared the sea of pirates," he replied, "but if the weather turns nasty in winter, the ships will not get through. It looks a bit risky. We do not have reserves for longer than a week, you know. I was talking to a fellow senator about it the other day and he appeared worried. You could build a new granary, and if the harvest failed and it was full of last year's surplus, you'd become a very rich woman – not that you aren't now," he said, looking a little embarrassed at his quip.

Lydia thought for a minute. "If we used more fields for the cultivation of cereals, and reduced some of the more luxury crops, we would have quite a surplus then. The population can't live on olives, but they need wheat and barley to make flour to keep them and their animals alive."

"That's right," said Gratius, "good thinking, why not have a chat with your managers and see what they say. After all, if there was a famine, they could lose their jobs anyway, but this way they wouldn't lose anything."

"Well I'd never get rid of them, come what may, but they would certainly have a poor time of it," replied Lydia.

A few days later Gratius arrived with his business partner Adonijah. He was a little bird-like man, with shrewd and sharp eyes that looked everywhere. Lydia took to him at once, almost as soon as he spoke to her, and welcomed him to her villa.

"I hope you will be able to answer some of my questions," she began with a smile. "Did Gratius give you any information about my trip to Judea? I didn't find out what I wanted to know, because I couldn't understand what I did hear and had no background knowledge of the Jewish race. If I can get that, then I might see where my experiences fit in, but I will not tell you what happened until I get the background." She laughed. "I know that sounds backwards but I don't want your personal feelings to get in the way. Does that make sense? I know it's a tall order but that's the way I want to find out, as I am totally perplexed."

"Of course, my lady," he replied. *He does have a charming voice*, she thought, *let's see how his brain works!*

"What I want is a short history of the Jewish race and of their Torah, and briefly what it says," said Lydia.

"Of course, my lady, I'll be only too pleased to help, but you must understand that a lot of it, being history, is often interpreted according to the thoughts and views of history teachers and historians in particular – but first I must state that, to the Jew, religion and politics are one and the same thing."

So he began by recounting as succinctly as possible the story of Prophet Abraham and the exodus from Egypt. Most of this was completely new to Lydia, steeped as she was in Roman and Greek history. She had no idea that the Jews had been slaves to the Egyptians for countless years, nor of their escape from slavery to the promised land. Adonijah then continued with more history and told of their god Yahweh, who they claimed was the maker and creator of everything. His instructions to the prophets and leaders of this new nation had been formulated to give the Jews direction and support, so long as they followed his rules – particularly when they were trekking through the desert when they escaped from Egypt. These rules were about personal behaviour, food, clothing, health – all things necessary to keep them together as an individual race in a hostile environment. But what interested Lydia most was that this god Yahweh was concerned with their welfare and promised to look after them so long as they obeyed his wishes. There was morality too in the fact that he insisted that they also cared for each other, which differed to most gods she had heard of, who were only interested in themselves. They spent their time fighting each other for supremacy, and when it all went wrong, it was the humans who got hurt!

So, continued Adonijah, as the law was laid down and recorded as the Torah, all appeared set for the Jews to become a great nation. When they settled in their promised land, it seemed that prosperity was theirs for the taking so long as they obeyed the law, but with prosperity came another generation who forgot all the rules and wanted to do it their way, and so it all fell apart.

Over the centuries Yahweh warned them again and again through his prophets that he would remove his care. Occasionally a leader emerged who encouraged this belief, but then the next generation found disaster when they ignored Yahwey's instructions, and so it went on. There was no stability, the rich remained rich, the poor starved, the dispossessed remained unloved, unwanted and abused – not a happy state and the people cried out in desperation for relief. Yahweh, through his prophets, told them that one day he would send his representative who would cleanse the nation of its ills and the nation would be reborn by 'he who was to come', the Messiah. The nation would be at the top table of the nations of the world once more, in fact the leader of the world, and a golden age would follow, where there would be no more pain, hunger, war or disease. The rest of the world would kneel at their feet; they were the chosen people, and let no one dispute it, or else.

Lydia listened to this tale and wondered, *Why do people behave so stupidly?* But she realised that that was what all nations did. This lot had a moral code that no other belief system had. It was unique, and to her wonderful to think that they could have a golden future if only they would listen. She then realised how it was that this preacher was condemned and that he was just one in a long line of others who had been got rid of simply for preaching that if people obeyed Yahweh's laws and cared for each other, there would be a golden age.

She said as much to Adonijah without mentioning the preacher by name, who said, "You're so right, my lady, and that's where it always goes wrong. When people only think of themselves, and when the leaders are also like that, what hope is there for the nation? But still we want the Messiah to come," he added with a rueful grin.

"So why do the present leaders still abuse anyone who questions their authority? After all, this generation has failed; it's occupied by Rome and that's not the freedom they want, is it? Is it because they think they have interpreted Yahweh's laws correctly? Because if they have, why are they not a free, independent nation?"

Adonijah shook his head. "Because any would-be dissident is a threat to those who have interpreted the law to their own advantage, with lies and half-truths. They do not follow the law in spirit, but in the letter, and in that lies injustice. Let me give you an example: no work is to be done on the Sabbath or it incurs a severe penalty, but everyone who has animals, even those in authority, have to go out each Sabbath to untie and feed them – that's work! But if, for example, a poor ill and starving man in the lower orders of society was seen picking an apple off a tree, he would be put before the judge for breaking the law for working on the Sabbath. He would be subject to the appropriate penalty and that would be severe!"

"Thank you, Adonijah," said Lydia. "It's basic politics then – no mercy, don't do as I do, but as I tell you. What a way to live!"

"You've got it, my lady," he replied.

So where does this Jesus, the Messiah as they call him, fit into all of this, Lydia thought. *After all, he was a Jew and, I was told, a practising one.*

She did not go into the interalia that night to pray to the household gods. She had come to realise it was a waste of time; lumps of stone do not give you any answers. They give you no direction, they don't care about you, and they fail to provide any support or comfort; it was just some whim of a storyteller.

As she slept, the voice came again. It was getting more frequent and insistent. "Lydia, your search will not be in vain, you will find me." She remembered the words as soon as she awoke. *They are becoming more relevant,* she thought. *Is it him? I'm beginning to think it is!"*

Gratius arrived later that day. "I'd like to talk about the granary idea," he began without any preamble. "I've been thinking about your idea of increasing your cereals on your farms and am thinking about doing it on mine. We could cooperate and build a huge granary, either here or on my estate. In the event of famine, and I think it may well come one day, we would be well protected from disaster. The emperor is not interested in anything to do with agriculture, but it will be his head on the block if he can't feed the plebs. So we need to get all your people together and use their expertise, plus that of the financial people. What do you think?"

"We need to think of the future, I agree," she answered him. "Don't forget though, you also have a family to consider but I'm on my own. I heard the other week that the only remaining relative of mine – my father's sister Aurelia in Herculaneum – died some years ago, which has been confirmed and the court has informed me she left nothing of value, so what of my future? Yes, I could get married again, but I'm no spring chicken and no man would want me – they would only for my money and I don't think I like the idea of that. My workers are my only family now! "But I need to do something with all my possessions and money. I'm going to tell you, if you will listen, what I learned from a very rich young Jewish man in Tiberius. I doubt you will agree with it, but it would solve my problems, and some that we have not thought of yet. Will you listen?"

"Alright," said Gratius laughing. "I will listen, and I promise you I will not interrupt , as I usually do!"

CHAPTER 12

Lydia sat on her patio by the pool deep in thought. She had spent the morning talking to her farm managers about the future of the estate and was pleased at their willingness to consider different ideas – some that she had put forward, and others that came from the men themselves. These, on the whole, were sensible suggestions.

The concept of a granary to store surplus grain was debated. The general consensus, when it was explained to them, was one of approval; they were aware of rising prices because of the thousands of extra mouths to feed in the city, and that it was becoming difficult to satisfy demand. Though the grain ships from Egypt were arriving regularly, all could see that this was, in reality, the weak link in the supply chain, and during war or bad weather, or due to other unknown factors, disaster and hunger could be just around the corner.

A few days earlier, she and Gratius had discussed the model of practice being used in Tiberius, but as he pointed out, it was one thing to antagonise a religious party regarding the ownership of property in a small impoverished country, but quite another to upset Rome, which, along with its environs was a large area farmed by a lot of very rich, influential people. As the price of grain increased because of the shortages, so these people got richer, and one must not forget that their taxes brought in more cash to keep the state afloat. A complete overhaul of the system would be unsettling, and there would be financial uncertainty, though both thought it an interesting idea., but it would take power from the rich and influential and hand it to those unused to business practices and so open to abuse. It should therefore be buried in the dustbin of history, as Gratius so elegantly put it!

They both accepted the idea of planning to increase the cereal crop at the expense of the luxury crops, and for a greater storage capacity to be made available. Lydia was looking forward to Gratius' visit next week when he would bring with him an engineer and financial expert to look in detail at the proposition.

It was pleasant sitting in the spring sunshine and she felt herself dozing off, when Cassius woke her saying, "My lady, Tribune Augustus is here to see you,with his wife and boys. Will you see them here or in the atrium?"

"Oh, show them in, I'll stay here," she replied. "How nice of them to call. It's a bit chilly for the pool, but I don't think the boys will mind!"

The tribune greeted Lydia with a smile, before introducing his wife, who appeared to be a somewhat reserved lady but joined in the conversation, mainly when it concerned family matters. The boys made a beeline for the pool, and ignoring the low temperature of the water jumped straight in with the maximum amount of noise and splashing. It seemed that they had settled for an afternoon of swimming and riding Cassius' very forgiving donkeys.

"You are off duty then?" observed Lydia, "For how long?"

Augustus laughed. "For not long enough," he replied, "but I'm glad to be away from the palace after the fuss of last week."

"Oh tell me about it," she said. "Bad, was it?"

"There's a small, quiet Jewish community in Rome," he began. "They have a little synagogue just down from the palace, which is run by a chap called Adonijah. He's not a rabbi, they have one of those as well, and he keeps out of the limelight. He'd be too obvious in his clerical garb and would attract a lot of attention, being an unusual sight in the city."

"Oh," exclaimed Lydia. "I know him, Gratius brought him to meet me last week to help me with a number of questions I wanted answering, he's a nice little man!"

"Well, he wasn't very nice last week," laughed Augustus. "He and his friends had some theological dispute with some new Jews to the area. He's a rich man, you know, who has his money in shipping. May I ask why he came to see you?"

"Of course. I wanted a short history of the Jewish people and Gratius said he would be a good source, and indeed he was, most informative! It was their Torah I wanted to know about, which contains all their rules and regulations, it was very interesting!"

"Oh I see," he replied. "Well apparently some immigrant Jews arrived from Judea – do you remember that preacher who healed my servant? – and they were followers of the movement called 'The Way'. Adonijah and his fellows threw them out in a theological dispute, and one or two hotheads started a fracas which spread. Everyone likes a riot, it doesn't matter what the cause is, there are people always ready for a punch up, which they think is fun! However, the noise upset the palace and we had to send a squad to sort it out. They arrested the wrong ones to start with, which added fuel to the flames and the rest is history. All riots follow a pattern, and we know on the whole how to sort it out, but it took a few days to calm it down and a few bloodied heads. A sorry-looking Adonijah was eventually hauled before the magistrates, where he apologized and promised to make his colleagues behave themselves in future. He was bound over to keep the peace and not to let it happen again, or else. The last thing those Jews needed was that sort of publicity.

"Anyway, these followers of 'The Way' say their leader, who they now call the Christos, is still alive and will come back soon to sort out the whole world, including Rome. That is causing comment in the corridors of power as well, so part of our remit now is to keep an eye on that lot also! But I assume old Adonijah couldn't stomach his authority being challenged by new ideas. It would be most unsettling to him, he's doing quite nicely out of Rome at present and wouldn't want anyone threatening that."

Lydia listened in silence, and thought, *It's spreading, and is now as far as Rome. Obviously there's some truth in it or it would have failed by now!*

"Thank you, Augustus," she replied. "That's one more piece added to the puzzle for me, most interesting, but look, time's getting on." She clapped her hands and Julia appeared, whereupon Lydia told her to arrange refreshments for her guests. Later that evening Augustus and his family left the villa, with the boys soaking wet having had a wonderful time, and the poor donkeys exhausted. Augustus' wife Lucia having found a friend in Lydia, and Augustus himself, having had time to relax for the first time that week, promised to come again on the insistent demands of their two sons.

Next morning, one of her managers arrived unexpectedly again to see her, "My lady," he started, "I hope you don't mind this intrusion, but I've been thinking about your suggestion of a granary. One of our fields is, and has always been to my knowledge, most unproductive for good crops. It's stony, but has a stream running next to it that has never dried up, and it's also near the main road. That field would be the ideal place to build the granary, and with the stream you could build a watermill next to it as well."

Lydia looked at him, smiled and nodded her head. "Now that is a very good idea, and we could mill our own grain as necessary. Would you need more staff?" she asked.

"I'm always in need of more staff," he laughed, "but now in particular. One of our new men, Joachim by name, he's a Jew from Judea, got beaten up by his fellows in an argument at their synagogue the other day – he got a clout round his head from something big and nasty. He'll be back to work soon I hope, but if you able to find me a replacement until he returns I'd be grateful. I wouldn't want to lose him though, he's a good worker."

"I'll come over and have a look in a couple of days. Senator Gratius is bringing an engineer and a banker to see me next week to discuss the project, so I'll have something to show him. Thank you, you've been most helpful, and I'll send another worker over tomorrow. It's good to know you're enthusiastic about this, as in the long run it will be of great benefit to us all. By the way, I would also like to talk to your man who got a clout on his head – that story rings a lot of bells in my head, as the clout probably did in his!"

It was two days before Lydia arranged to get to the farm where the proposed granary would be built. The details had already been worked out by the manager, Marius, and she was greatly impressed by his grasp of the project. He was an ex–army man who had been demobilised after being wounded in a skirmish with some rebels in Tuscany a few years ago. As a senior non-commissioned officer he had been taught not only fighting skills, but also masonry for bridges, general building and roads, and this previous army training had stayed with him into civilian life. Her father had taken pity on him one day when he came to the estate looking for work. It was with some surprise, however, that Lydia found her manager had committed his plans to scrolls; she had not realised he could read and write, which was another legacy from his army days. She recalled that her father had been a good judge of character, and all those he had employed for management positions had proved worthy of their calling.

When they got into conversation following her perusal of his plans, she asked him if he read anything. He replied that he liked to get hold of any work of philosophy if he could. They talked of this for a while, and she offered him the use of her small library if he would like to come over sometime. "I would appreciate that very much, my lady," he replied with a surprised smile.

Lydia next wanted to talk to the worker who had

been injured in the fracas at the synagogue and she found him at work in the stable brushing down a mule.

"Ah, Joachim, can I have a chat with you?" she asked.

He was reluctant to talk to her at first as she was his employer and also a woman, but when she assured him that she meant him no harm and would not repeat their conversation to the manager, he relaxed somewhat. She told him that she was interested in talking to people involved in the Jewish movement now called 'The Way', and that she had lived in Judea and had knowledge of the country and of the itinerant preacher called Jesus of Nazareth. He smiled at this and gave her his full attention. She told him about her friend the tribune whose servant had been healed, and Joachim said he knew of that episode because it had happened in his village, and he also knew of the officer.

"Was his name Augustus?" he asked.

"That's right," she cried. "You were there! Oh this is wonderful, so you know all about it?"

"The man who was cured was my cousin," he said.

"What a really small world," replied Lydia with delight. "Do you mind if I come and talk to you again?"

"Of course not, my lady, I'd be pleased to talk to you, but you know there are things I don't understand about it all. We have been told that he really is the Messiah, which I do believe, but he's not the Messiah talked about in the books." He frowned. "I want to believe it, because they say he's coming again, and soon."

Lydia smiled. "Yes I've heard that and this is what I want to find out. By the way, did you know Simon Peter in Gallilee?"

"Oh yes, he's known as Cephas now I understand, and was given that name by the Master. I know the whole family, nice people, " he replied.

"I heard him talk in Jerusalem," Lydia told him, "most impressive and I would like to have heard more. It's difficult for me to understand your idea of one god, because us Romans have hundreds of gods. It's taking me a long while, but I'm slowly coming round to your concept of monotheism. There is something about this that doesn't quite add up though, and I need to find out answers. Thank you for talking to me."

She returned to her manager Marius. "I'll be back with the senator next week," she said, "and hopefully we will get things under way, but keep those details you have recorded; they are first class and I must congratulate you on them. I'm sure the senator will be as impressed as I am." The manager bowed, a look of pleasure suffusing his face. "Thank you, my lady," he replied, "you are most kind."

Lydia went to bed that night and thought about her conversation with Joachim. He had seemed to believe in the fact that this itinerant preacher who healed Augustus' servant was the Messiah, the one promised to save Israel, but the preacher hadn't come up to his measure of what the Torah said. The trouble was that there was not, nor had there ever been, so far as she could discover, any discussion of the Torah. There was such a rigid adherence to the stated text; you were not allowed to question it, this was what it said, and it meant what it said, and that was the end of it. Now the followers of 'The Way' were behaving in the same pattern. They believed they were right, ergo others must be wrong – no meeting of minds there.

"Think again, Lydia," came the voice like a bolt from the blue.

Startled, she sat up in bed and had a drink of water. As she lay back again, her mind continued its thought process. Traditionally they seem to expect that this Messiah will come to save them from others, but perhaps that's the problem, and they've missed the point. He will surely instead be coming to save them from themselves, their mulish stupidity and obstinacy. Of course! She smiled and went straight to sleep.

The following week, the senator and his associates visited Lydia at the villa, and after a brief discussion went over to the farm in question. They looked at the position, road access and suitability of the land for building purposes, and after a review of Marius' proposals, of which Gratius heartily approved, thought that the idea of the watermill would be good for business. After inspecting the area, they retired to the farm manager's office, and over a large jug of wine, looked at the present position regarding the type and value of crop, and the prospects of this year's harvest and income. They also took into account occurrences that would derail their plans, such as the occasional outbreaks of plague, pestilence and stormy weather.

Eventually, after looking at every possibility, they agreed a plan that was viable to be put into action as soon as the harvest was in. Gratius had brought a number of scribes with him to document the plans, so that each person involved could be given a copy. They planned then to get together after harvest and review it in the light of existing circumstances before the work started.

So the day–to–day work went on and Lydia went to bed each night exhausted. It was the busiest time of the year in farming and contracts had to be signed with various commercial and government bodies for the supply of grain and other farm produce. These needed attention to detail as they required a lot of her business acumen, but Lydia was fortunate in that Cassius, who had been with her father for many years, and had been his right-hand man, knew much of what was required to keep the estate in good order and profitable. Although she employed temporary staff to scribe, they also needed supervision, and Cassius demonstrated his ability to deal with and manage them.

Little of the outside world impinged on Lydia's life at these times, as she was kept so busy keeping the business going. She had another conversation with Joachim, who was now recovered from his beating, but was unable to get any further with her questions. It seemed that all the followers of 'The Way' had been seduced by the idea that the end of the world was coming, that the Master would come again in glory, and that they would all be given thrones and crowns of gold and harps to play on – or whatever they thought had been promised.

Lydia felt that the whole thing was becoming a chimera, and would all disappear in a cloud of misery. The followers were not working for the day–to–day things of life and trying to improve them, like living in peace and harmony with each other, which the Master had demanded they should do, but were instead looking for liberation in heaven from their unfulfilled lives. If they wanted to change their lives, as she had thought the other night, they should be attempting to gain liberation from themselves and their obstinate ideology, then they could start thinking how they might achieve heaven on earth. Now that was certainly a message that appealed to her!

Meanwhile, Gratius was a tower of strength and his advice was proving to be invaluable. However, the last time he had come to see how the arrangements were coming along, he had said he was worried and told Lydia of the problem the Senate was having with Emperor Claudius. Once or twice, so far as he knew, Claudius had sidelined the Senate when cases of malfeasance on the part of some well-connected people had occurred. The emperor had settled these himself in private, which was said to have been his advantage, instead of hauling them before the courts, with the fines going to the treasury. A further problem was that important decision–making had been handed over to some newly–arrived Greek immigrants, wealthy ones of course, and they always arranged things to the emperor's advantage, thus creating an atmosphere at the palace. These same Greek men were often accompanied by their pretty boyfriends, and this stuck in the craw of the more conservative senators!

However, the general feeling of discontent had been brought to the attention of the emperor, and he was now looking for something to distract opinion away from himself, to restore his popularity with some major policy change, and to take minds away from his peccadilloes.

"It will, in all probability, cost us dear," said Gratius glumly. "It is rumoured he is considering some military campaign to get more territory. Which means more expense – and of course, we will pay in increased taxes."

When Gratius visited again two months later, as the harvest was being completed, he told Lydia that Claudius was planning to invade Britain in the spring. He was busy building a large invasion fleet in Gaul, and the army was being moved up to the north coast in readiness.

"This is going to cost a lot of money, so we'd better get going as quickly as possible with our plans, before we get taxed to the hilt in order to keep that cross-eyed idiot on the throne," he grumbled.

"Do they ever learn?" asked Lydia. "It's time we had a different form of government, where the emperor is accountable to the Senate – rather than him thinking everyone is accountable to him."

"Yes, that would be ideal," replied Gratius.

And so later that year, it was learned that the armyhad been moved north in readiness for the invasion. The Praetorian Guard would accompany the emperor personally so that Claudius did not get hurt in the fighting with tribesmen – no glory in that for him was the general consensus! He wanted to get back to Rome and have a huge triumph and cement himself into the glorious history of the Empire!

CHAPTER 13

The work began in the early part of the winter, after all the crops were in. Marius suggested that it was important to firstly get to work on the watermill, which would need to have a dam built behind it to ensure a steady flow of water. Had only the stream been used, there would have been an insufficient supply of water to turn the wheel, particularly at the end of a dry summer, and a millpond created by the dam would also give a reasonable and workable head of water at all times. Marius was used to this sort of problem–solving exercise, and as he explained the theories and practicalities to Lydia, she was again impressed by her father's choice of his work force; he had not only a good idea about human nature, but also an awareness of the technical expertise needed to go with the job.

There was plenty of unquarried stone available; the stream flowed downhill on the estate into a small and rocky valley, too barren to grow anything, before it finally plunged into the sea some miles away. The stream could become a raging torrent after the winter snow and rain, and to avoid damage to the mill, a sluice was needed to bypass the mill and take the excess melt water away from the building, thus preventing their work being swept into the valley and ensuring there was a constant water supply to the mill, irrespective of the weather.

Lydia had to employ two more labourers from the

village to assist Marius. Joachim was taken from his position caring for the mules to help with the quarrying of stone; he had done the same work when living in Judea, when he had worked on the Roman palace there, and had a good eye for building materials. Marius, as an ex–army man,was not only skilled in masonry, but also possessed good management skills. The four men made a good and efficient team, and the work progressed well. Within four months, the buildings, millpond and the sluice were ready, and they were also ready to fit the water wheel and the millstones, which would mill the grain. The millstones had to be purchased ready–dressed from Italian Gaul, and Gratius used his business expertise to source suitable stones for the project, which were to be delivered as soon as possible, in order to arrive before the completion of the harvest.

So, the work progressed well. The mill and its outbuildings, the mill pond and sluices were in place before summer arrived, and the granary was ready two months later. The project was completed on time, which was a great credit to Marius' organization, and Lydia and Gratius congratulated him on a job well done!

The new range of crops had more emphasis on grain rather than on luxury items, although the vines for wine, olives and fruit trees were to lesser extent, still farmed. As Marius pointed out, in the lean years – and they would come he predicted – it was grain that would be the staple crop to keep the population and the animals alive, and grain only required drying, whist the other method of preserving of food was by salting. That was not very practicable for fruit, although some vegetables such as beans could be salted.

Lydia worked hard all winter with all the usual business problems, and the many changes planned incurred a lot more work, but it was an interesting time for her and she became better acquainted with her staff. She liked to talk to them, when they could spare the time, about their families. The men were a little hesitant to do this at first, but eventually became used to this patrician lady talking to them at their level.

Hearing stories of their family problems, Lydia tried to help them as much as she could, and invited the wives and children of the workers to the villa for some light refreshments and a chat. She enjoyed these times immensely, being herself childless. The children had a great time in the pool, and playing with Cassius' donkeys, and the mothers never left without a basket of fruit or some treats for the children. It was amazing how much good will this mill project had generated and how it had opened Lydia's eyes to the plight of working people. She found their whole lives were lived on a knife's edge, with hunger and disease and more unwanted pregnancies than were planned for, or could be afforded.

Augustus' wife Lucia was becoming a frequent visitor, with Augustus away with the army for the invasion of Britain. She brought her boys with her, who could indulge their high spirits to their heart's content on the estate. They were fascinated with all the work going on, and Lucia and Lydia often took them over to see the work on the millpond, which was filling day–by–day. However, the men were afraid for the boys safety and spent time keeping them out of mischief! But a good time was had, and Lucia reveled in Lydia's friendship. She felt at home in her company and was grateful to have someone with whom to share her anxieties.

One day Lucia asked Lydia, when the boys were outside playing with the donkey, how it was that she Lydia never seemed to worry, living as she did as a woman in a man's world, with problems both domestic and business to contend with. She said it seemed that Lydia glided serenely through life without a care in the world and that she envied her composure.

"Don't forget," replied Lydia laughing, but pleased with the compliment, "as a service wife for years, you have to take it all on the chin. As you know, we were at the very seat of power, and I learned early on that I had to keep my thoughts to myself and not interfere with my husband's judgements. His worries made mine pale into insignificance. Unlike you, we did not spend a lot of time apart, and I had to share his problems without being too involved. I couldn't afford to be judgemental; he was the one who made the major decisions and our life had to fit in around them. Most of those decisions were often bigger ones than I would have wanted to take, literally being decisions of life and death."

"Yes, we've had a fair number of separations since we were married," said Lucia, "and we've just had to get on with it. I have never stopped worrying about him and the boys, though this latest one, to this dreadful island Britain, which is full of the most savage tribes on record I hear, who make the most cruel opponents."

Lydia thought for a moment, then decided to tell Lucia about the voice. She felt that she was always under some sort of guidance and did nothing in isolation, so went on to tell her of the man in her dream and his promise that he would always be with her, right through to her husband's death and beyond. She explained that she felt that somebody seemed to know all her cares and woes, and this was, she knew, where her strength lay, and would one day help her to find the truth.

Lucia listened carefully, it took time in the telling, but when Lydia had finished, she asked, "When did you last hear the voice?"

"A few days ago," she replied, and explained about Joachim and his quest for the answers in life. She also explained that she thought it that this 'Christos' could be the spectre that had come to her, but she needed to know more than that.

Lucia said thoughtfully, "You know, this is exactly what I want. I've got the household gods, but they do nothing for me if I'm worried. They're alright if all is well and I give thanks to them, but do they really do anything for me? I don't think they do."

"I quite agree," replied Lydia. "We are sold these ideas to keep us quiet I think! They don't help though, do they? I need to know more. There are a few in Rome who knew this Christos when he was alive, and they tell of some of his teachings. From what I know about him, he was quite a wonderful person, but he's dead now. However, these people say he is alive, and I think it's his voice I hear. I have no proof at all though, I shall have to explore further when all the building work is finished and go to Rome on some pretext to try and find out. But you know," she said rather hesitantly, "I'm beginning to find that when I do have problems – and believe me I do – it is in helping others that I resolve my own. How does that sound to you, Lucia?"

"Yes, that sounds right to me," she replied thoughtfully. "Well I think I understand you a lot better after today, thank you, Lydia."

Lydia glanced up at the sun. "It's getting late, and I'm famished. You'll stay and have a bite, won't you?"

Lydia clapped her hands and Julia appeared, "Can we feed these hungry mortals tonight?" she asked.

"Of course, my lady," replied Julia. "I'll get the cook to organise it. We've got some fresh fish, would you all like that?"

"Oh lovely," said Lucia, "we love fish. We can't get a lot round here. We always had fish at home when I was a girl, and I do miss it We knew a lot of fishermen and father would let them take we children out in the boats sometimes, they were rough men but so nice to us."

"The Christos' friends were all fishermen," said Lydia. "They've got a lot of patience, I'm told, and I believe they have, but you're right, we don't get a lot of fish around here being inland. The Tiber is so dirty I doubt they could live in it." She then paused a moment before she cried, "Of course! Why don't I get Marius to put some fish in the new millpond, they'd live in that. It's lovely clean mountain water, and we could have the freshest fish in this part of the world! Yes, I'll ask him next week on my next visit to the mill."

When Lydia visited the mill site the following week, she mentioned to Marius the idea of fish in the millpond.

"I don't really know, my lady," he replied. "It's rather small for a sustainable catch. Let me think about it if you will."

The work was almost completed: the buildings were

finished and the mill stones fitted, the gears had been tested and had been found to work well, with only a few snags to be ironed out. Marius had reported this to Lydia, when one morning he had arrived unexpectedly at the villa.

"I've been thinking about fish, my lady," he began, "and I've had a brain wave!"

"Let's hear it then," said Lydia, laughing at the serious look on his face, "I hope it's a good one!"

"Well, my lady, the millpond is rather small, so you need something bigger. We also need to ensure a good supply of fish, which is expensive to buy. However, if we bred enough fish, we could make a good profit selling the surplus. Also, in the event of crop failure, we would still have a food supply," he replied.

"So what is your brainwave then? It sounds alright so far."

"This is rather a big idea," he began hesitantly, "but where the stream leaves the mill, having ground our cereals, it flows into that rocky valley which is no good for anything. We can't plant in it, so why not dam it, make a lake and fill it with thousands of fish?" He looked at her sheepishly.

Lydia stared back at him for a moment, then a grin spread across her face. "What a marvellous idea!" she cried. "You're right, it's no good for anything, Marius, you are a genius! I'll talk to Gratius about it to arrange finance and breeding stocks. He'll know just what to do, and when it's done, we'll call it Lake Marius!"

Marius burst out laughing. "Well I never expected to have a lake named after me! That would be wonderful, what a thing to tell my grandchildren! Thank you, my lady."

The harvest came and went. It was very fruitful this year and after all the contracts had been fulfilled, there was a surplus of approximately one quarter of the whole crop, which was stored in the new granary. Lydia had employed a man to supervise the granary; he reported directly to Marius and had a knowledge of crop storage. He knew how to maintain its quality for possibly a number of years in store, and that some of the crop would be needed as seed for next year's planting in the spring, so on the whole she and Marius were pleased with the progress made so far.

The mill was proving to be just as successful. Some local farmers had brought their grain for milling as the word spread, as otherwise the process of milling was a time-consuming and inefficient method done using hand equipment. It seemed that the mill would pay for itself within three harvests.

The dam project for 'Lake Marius' was well into the planning stage and Marius had surveyed the area and located the best stone for its construction. He wanted to make a masonry frame and fill it with earth, and when digging the earth out of the proposed lake bed to deepen the valley, he had discovered more useful stone for future building purposes. The deepening of the lake bed would increase the amount of stored water, and so hopefully would allow a larger amount of fish to breed in its depths, with the deeper water being cooler, and thus more beneficial to the breeding process. It was planned that as soon as harvest was over, the work on the dam could start. Winter was approaching, and the quarrying and earth excavation would be easier to deal with in cooler weather.

Gratius thought the whole idea was a very good

business proposition and accepted the task of sourcing fish with which to start stocking the lake when it was filled. The source had to be reasonably local so that getting the fish to the lake in good condition would be possible, and fortunately Gratius located a source in a river in the hills that was abounding with trout. He also wanted carp, a fish much prized for its firm flesh, but most of this type of fish seemed to be the property of private land owners, who did not feel inclined to part with any of their favourite fish to start a shoal in somebody else's lake.

Gratius thought the naming of the lake was a wonderful idea; he had come to respect Marius' expertise since he had been associated with Lydia's projects, and thought this was an excellent way to repay him for all his hard work – not only on the lake project but also on the mill, which he knew was working admirably.

Lucia's two boys were intrigued to have the lake in their vicinity, and were told by Marius that they would be able to fish in it. They were also told by Lydia, to shouts of delighted approval, that she would get a boat they could use which to their heart's content when the lake filled.

"Will it have sails?" asked Gauis, the older of the two boys.

"But of course," replied Lydia, "and oars, and I'll teach you how to sail it." Lydia was an accomplished sailor and swimmer, having lived by the sea for the first years of her life.

The dam was completed the following spring. As the water flowed into it, they stood in wonderment and watched the barren valley transform itself into a lovely blue lake. It reflected the hills above the farm, and water birds began to arrive and find a home there. Gratius had found a stock of fish, though instructions were given that none were to be taken the first year so as to allow the waters to mature and the fish to grow and breed.

Although they tried to keep the lake private for the time being, and for the use of Lydia's staff alone, two poachers were apprehended attempting to get at the fish stocks. The two wretched youngsters were brought before Lydia, roped together by a most displeased Marius. They were from the local village – Julia said she knew them, they were both orphans who had lost their parents a few years ago from the plague outbreak. They were a sorry, scruffy-looking pair, obviously starving and dressed in rags. She had them locked in an outhouse for a night after giving them the best meal they had had for weeks, judging by the way they ate it. She could have handed them over to the magistrates, but she knew that had she done so, they would have been flogged to within an inch of their lives and probably injured in both body and spirit. Her heart went out to them, so she went to bed that night to sleep on it and decide what to do with them in the morning.

However, the voice woke her again in the early morning. "Lydia, you love your fellow men, never give up." *These messages are getting personal,* she thought, *I do feel I'm being watched, but it is a gentle voice and somewhat comforting.*

She later awoke to the sounds of the birds on a lovely

spring morning. After breakfast she found Cassius in the atrium filling the flower pots with cuttings of summer flowering plants. *He's got green fingers,* she thought. There was something about the man; everything he did, he did it well. *He's just one of those people who excel at whatever they put their hand to.*

Lydia asked him what he thought of the lake and whether he had been over to the valley to see the work in progress.

"Oh yes, my lady," he replied. "It looks so calm and peaceful. What is it about water that is so soothing to the soul?"

"Do you know of anyone with carpentry skills who could make a small boat, but big enough to carry four people?" she asked him. "The boys would love that, and it would teach them discipline if they learnt to sail."

"Indeed I do, my lady, I have a friend who is a carpenter and another who is a boatwright, I'll speak to them both for you and see what they can do."

Suddenly she remembered the two young poachers in the shed and sent for them. After a few words of admonishment from Lydia, they had the grace to apologise and promised not to repeat their wrongdoing. They were starving, they said, and were grateful that they had not been sent to the magistrate, where they knew they would have been flogged.

Lydia looked at these two rootless boys, little older than Augustus' two, and her heart went out to them again. What hope had they in this world, with no role model, and no ability to feed themselves apart from thieving? The lower orders of society had few prospects; most families had a hard job feeding their own children and would not want to have extra mouths to feed from somebody else's family– and two teenagers would eat a lot of food. She remembered the voice from the night before, and realized that she couldn't just throw them out!

"Would you like to work for me?" she asked. The boys looked at her, surprised. "I'll feed you in return for your labour, but you will have to prove yourselves. Are you good at anything?"

The oldest boy said he was interested in masonary and the younger said he liked farm work.

"Well, you come to work for me and we will see in a few weeks if you are good enough. You will be with Marius, who brought you to me last night, as he's the farm manager. Do as you are told or the magistrate will deal with you, will you do that?"

"Yes, my lady," they chorused.

Lydia went on, "Marius will find you somewhere to live and will see that you get regular meals and we will talk about pay later, if you are suitable. In the meantime, here is Marius. Now go with him and he will tell you what to do."

"Thank you, my lady," said the older one whilst the younger one was by now in tears!

They then trotted off with the manager, who was not overly pleased to have the two rascals under his care, though they would be two useful lads for fetching and carrying things for the other workers.

Cassius looked at her. "I hope, my lady, those two don't let you down," he said solemnly.

Lydia replied, "They're just two starving children; I can't throw them out when we live in plenty. We must help those less able to help themselves where we can, or they will help themselves to what we have!" she laughed.

"You're too kind, my lady. You are, if I may say so, a true chip off the old block!"

Cassius was as good as his word and one afternoon brought his friend the carpenter to see Lydia. The carpenter told her that Cassius had given him the details of the small boat required and agreed to build one for her. The price was negotiated and he told her his friend the boatwright was available, and they would start work on it as soon as reasonably possible.

"Can we sail it on our own?" asked Gaius.

"Indeed you can, but you will need to have some instruction first. I don't think your father would be very pleased if I let you go out in it on your own without knowing what to do properly," she replied. "I'll instruct you, so you can learn how to raise and lower the sails. I know all about boats because I was brought up with them."

By this time, Lucia and the boys were virtually part of her family, and the boys now referred to her as Aunt Lydia, which gave her a lot of pleasure. The younger one, Lucius, found it difficult at first, but eventually came round to it on the promptings of his mother.

The boat was eventually delivered at the beginning of spring and was painted white and red at the request of the boys. On the first trip, Lydia skulled the boat out into deep water before raising the sails, and being a windy day the boat danced across the water to the delight of the boys. It gave great satisfaction to Lydia to see these two lads enjoying themselves so much, as both were missing their father, who was away on active service.

After a series of lessons, Lydia felt they were competent enough to go on their own, and for the rest of the spring and summer they spent many happy hours on board when not at their studies. Their tutor found it difficult to keep their minds on Latin and Greek verbs when he was with them, but did remark to Lucia how much brighter they seemed with this new interest. He even permitted himself a sail in their boat and was quite impressed at their acquired skills, and congratulated Lydia on the quality of her teaching!

One evening as they were approaching the landing stage, built for them by the two poacher boys on Marius' instructions, an argument developed between the two about how one should approach with a side wind. Gaius grabbed the tiller out of the hand of Lucius, forcing the boat to slew round. The boom swung and knocked Lucius into the water, and he went under straightaway.

Joachim, who had been waiting to pull the boat out of the water, leant over the side of the jetty to catch hold of Lucius' shirt, which was just showing. Seeing what was happening, Gaius pushed him out of the way and jumped in to get hold of his brother. Meanwhile Joachim missed his handhold on the jetty, fell into the lake and floundered into deep water. Unfortunately, although brought up on the lake side in Gallilee, he could not swim, and disappeared. The boat drifted away and Gaius dragged his brother to shore. By the time he had run to fetch Marius, Joachim was nowhere to be seen, and was not discovered until the next morning, face down in the water.

Lydia was devastated. When the boys eventually owned up to arguing when in charge of a boat they received a dressing-down from Lydia.

"Look what your arguing achieved," she stormed at them. "Your behaviour was totally irresponsible, and I hope you can now see the consequences of indiscipline whilst sailing. It is a serious business, as this dreadful episode proves. I don't know how you are going to come to terms with this."

"But he was only a labourer," Gaius said truculently.

"That, young man," exploded Lydia, "is the most wicked remark I have ever heard. You should be thoroughly ashamed of yourself. He was a fellow human being, and a husband and a father. Would you like to go down to the village now and tell them that by your stupidity and irresponsibility his wife is now a widow, and his three children are fatherless? How are they now to get enough food to eat? Would you like to do that? And while we are at it, Joachim died trying to save the life of your small brother. I hope you will always remember that."

When Joachim's wife was told she was distraught. How was she going to survive without her husband and with four mouths to feed? Lydia brought her up to the villa and spent the rest of the day trying to give her some comfort, reassuring her that she would always be in Lydia's thoughts and that she would do the best for her and see that she came to no harm.

Joachim was buried the next day as required by Jewish law, and Lydia made sure that everyone on the estate attended, in particular Gaius, so he would see the misery and realize that through his thoughtlessness he had helped to cause the tragedy. Joachim's wife had some relatives in Rome who, like Joachim, were followers of 'The Way', and she was assured they would take them in and care for them. So Lydia took charge of all the arrangements for their move to the capital and decided to go herself and see them settled in.

Before they went, she wanted, with Gaius' mother's agreement, for the boy to speak with Joachim's wife and offer his sincere condolences. Both Lydia and Lucia felt that because he was almost a man by law, he should act like one as a necessary part of growing up and face the world as it really was. Born with a silver spoon in his mouth, he needed to be made aware of the plight of the average working family, who lived on a knife edge of poverty, with disease, starvation and homelessness a constant threat to their everyday lives.

It had been some years since she had been to the capital even to visit her properties, and she was amazed at the development she found. The city boundaries had extended considerably and much of it was unknown to her now, but they found the home of Joachim's kin in a poor apartment block, shared with four other families – all followers of 'The Way', she was informed. After the family had settled in, Lydia was asked if she would like to share their evening meal, as it would be well after dark by the time her transport got her home. "Thank you, my friends," she replied, "that is kind of you, yes I would like that very much."

She was surprised to find that all of the four families in the block would be eating together. "We always do," one of them said to her, "not only is it good fellowship, but it's more economical."

As all were followers of 'The Way', the oldest man present asked them all to stand to offer a prayer to the Christos before the meal, asking him to bless the food they were eating, and thanking him for his goodness to them in providing another day's work. To her amazement and some discomfort, the old man also gave thanks for sending lady Lydia among them at this sad time with her words of comfort.

This was the first time she had met such a number of the followers of 'The Way' and she was intrigued. The food was poor but well served, and she felt completely at home with them. They were the most unselfish people she had ever met, and were very different to so many of her fellow citizens. They were all so convinced that their Christos would return at any moment that they had to be prepared for this happening at any time of the day or night, and they would then get their reward in the wonderful world they expected him to create.

Lydia listened to all their expectations. They sat there as they told her of it with such honest and shining faces that she felt she could not speak any argument against what she felt was an unrealistic aspiration. Indeed they all appeared to be poorly educated and were unable to even counter a simple question or argument except to say "Well that's what the Master said would happen!" However, seeing the peace and harmony in this little group, she felt that if nothing else it was a lesson to all on how to live in social harmony and equality, and was wonderful training in good social behaviour.

But as she travelled back to the villa that night, and relaxed on the cushions of her conveyance, another question troubled her. If, as they claimed, their Master was the son of God, why did he allow himself to be killed in the first place? Yes, those good people had a lot more than most people, rich or poor, because they had peace of mind, and the expectation of heaven on earth, with a future in a heavenly kingdom assured, and for people in their position in life, this was an enviable situation to be in – yet to get this, their leader had to be executed. It didn't make sense; there must be someone, somewhere, who had the answer. *But where do I find him?* she thought. *I can't help but feel that they have somehow got it right, and I want it as well!*

CHAPTER 14

The year passed quickly and Augustus' two boys had had a wonderful year until the dreadful death of Joachim. Gaius thereafter became a more thoughtful young man and had come to terms with the fact that he had contributed to the labourer's death. He spoke no more, at least not in Lydia's hearing, in a disparaging way about working people, realising it was them who provided him with all the services he enjoyed, and it was them who permitted him to live the comfortable life to which he had always felt he was entitled by right.

Lydia was pleased with this transformation, and Lucia and she discussed how difficult it was to bring up a young man today with the prevailing social mores. But as Lydia pointed out, she had heard the same sentiments expressed by her father, and was sure that her grandfather, and indeed his father before him, had said the same thing!

One year the winter was very wet and cold and the lake filled to overflowing. Marius worried about the strength of the dam walls, but he had done his work well and it held under the huge pressure of water. His other worry was that all the fish could have been washed away, but it proved to be an unnecessary fear, as the shoals remained intact and appeared to thrive.

It would soon be planting time again; the granary had ample stores for the seeding of the fields, and they all looked forward to another good harvest. But as was well known in country circles, a cold and wet winter did not always lead to the required warm and dry spring , and the coldness continued well into mid –year. Sown crops were washed away and the fields became waterlogged and unproductive, with a resulting total failure of the grain and vegetable harvest. To add to the problem, the grain ships had not only been held up with bad weather, but the yield in the Egyptian provinces was also at a record low. It looked as though Gratius' prognostication of famine looked a distinct possibility.

Claudius, following his martial success in Britain, held a huge triumph in Rome at the turn of the year, extravagantly depleting the food stocks of the city by giving free handouts of food that would have helped them through the next years. The prospect of food riots was now very likely as prices soared and supplies dwindled, and with it came ill health and disease, affecting the young, old and sick in particular. The plebs and slaves at the bottom of the social scale were going to bed hungry at night and waking the next morning to a another day of starvation .

As Gratius remarked on one of his visits to the estate, "Common sense was never the way of Rome's emperors, their guiding light seems to be selfish behaviour and pride, and pride always comes before a fall. We are now in for a bad time for the next few years. It takes only a few months for a food shortage to develop, but the resulting deaths from starvation and the subsequent disease takes years to work itself out of the system. This is what happens when emperors take their eye off the ball when all is going well."

Already the cost of staple foodstuff was rising rapidly, and the threat of social discord was being heard. In the villages, the occupants were aware of the problems of food production and had various ways of turning to other types of food for sustenance, but the plebs and the myriads of slaves in Rome were set to be very annoyed with the authorities when they found even more shortages and no alternatives to their diet. By the end of the year the whole country was in a state of famine, then plague struck and other conditions of malnutrition, and the populace was unable to develop any resistance to these diseases which took off the young, the old and the chronically sick.

Lydia, with the willing help of Lucia and Cassius, arranged the distribution of food to the local villagers from her granary. Gratius remarked, "A very wise move of yours, Lydia, building that store. At least we won't go without."

Lydia replied tartly, "It's not 'we' that I'm concerned about, but the poor villagers down the road; the women and children and our estate workers who all live there. They are the ones who need my care and I've already put a plan into action to get food to them. I am discussing with Cassius this evening how we are going to do it fairly."

Lydia felt that all her workers and their families were her responsibility at this threatening time, and knew it was going to take a lot of work to ensure a fair supply of food to them. A fair supply would mean that heavy manual workers got more than the clerical workers, and pregnant women got more than others, and so on.

Gracius looked suitably chastised at her words.

"You're a remarkable woman, Lydia," he said contritely. "I've never met anyone like you before!"

Lydia settled down for the night, exhausted at her day's work. As she settled the voice came again. "Lydia, you will find me. You are not far from me."

For the first time, she felt she had to answer back. "But who are you? Are you the one who is to come?"

There was silence, and then she heard the wind suddenly gust and a sharp splatter of rain fall on the bedroom shutter. "Don't look for another kingdom, it's within you," said the voice faintly, and then it was gone.

When she awoke the next morning, the sun was shining for the first time in days. It was a watery sun indeed, but none the less pleasant for all that. She thought of the voice last night. She felt reassured to some extent but was still puzzled; was it he who 'The Way' followers called the Master? He sounded so down to earth and immediate to her, not like the Master the followers seemed to believe in, with promises of wonderful worlds to come and being free from oppression. For her it was just getting on with the job, not fantasizing about what you will get out of it if you behave in a certain way! *There's no time for that,* she thought. *People need care now, not food tomorrow!*

So the relief system went into action the next day with the distribution of grain as required, and fortunately plenty of fish. Marius' fears had proved unfounded, the fish stocks were high, although fresh meat was in short supply, and fish supplemented the locals' diet. Every little helped at this time of shortage, and so they survived until the following spring when fresh planting took place with the stored grain saved from distribution by Cassius' careful planning. There had been, thanks to adequate feeding, no more than the usual winter health problems, and they now had the prospect of a better year ahead as the normal weather for the time of year returned.

Augustus, Lucia's husband, returned from the conquest of Britain. He'd been congratulated by the emperor himself on his prowess in battle, but having been on garrison duties for a year after the conquest, he wondered when he would see home again! To the great relief of Lucia, he arrived safely one morning. The boys were overjoyed at his homecoming; they had missed him terribly and were delighted to take their father to the lake a few days later and show him their expertise in sailing. Lucia, however, insisted that Gauis told his father about the death of Joachim and his part in the dreadful event.

Augustus listened carefully to his report and said, "Well, now you know. It's called responsibility; think before you act."

"That's what mother said," he replied. "I've changed my mind about a lot of things since then," he said ruefully, and went on to tell his father how he would like to join the army when he was old enough.

Augustus nodded approval. "You'll have to get used to being with a lot of people at all times, and if you are to become an officer, learn all about them and their needs. You must also learn to lead from the front, so that you can lead a team. The Roman Army is all about teamwork, and hard physical labour, believe me, but it's most rewarding. It's about responsibility, giving and taking orders, and having pride in what you are doing. Don't ever forget, the Roman Army is the finest in the world. You'll do alright so long as you remember that."

"Thank you, Father," he replied,"I won't forget"

So the good weather returned and seed planting went ahead, but in the towns and cities there were gaps in the population as many had succumbed to the famine and disease. Lydia realised that her granary had been responsible for saving many lives and planned to extend the storage facilities to take a bigger capacity. What she had done had just managed to avoid disaster, but had the weather continued to be inclement for another year, they would have been in real trouble. She knew she must have at least two years' supply in hand in the future. The clue was in well-husbanded farms, good quality and adequate storage facilities, and now she and her managers had to get on with the work rapidly.

Cassius remarked to her one day, when in a reflective mood, "You know, my lady, we have been blessed on this estate thanks to your wisdom. Isn't it strange how out of such sorrow and loss of your dear ones, so much good has come?"

Lydia thought for a moment. "I've been more than blessed," she replied smiling, "I think my life has been directed since those days, and the man with the voice who comes to me is really the one responsible."

"What man?" asked Cassius, looking puzzled. "I didn't know about that, my lady."

"Well, perhaps it's time you did," she replied."Not a lot of people know this, so I'll tell you."

The planting had gone well and all the post-winter chores on the estate were completed. The boys were back on the lake again with their boat, enjoying the windy weather and life to the full. Marius had taught them to fish with a rod and line and was also teaching them archery and use of a cross bow, which he told Gaius would be a useful skill if he wanted to join the army – as a fighting soldier he would be expected to be expert in the use of both types of weapon. Both boys were now getting target practice regularly, and to the extreme annoyance of Gauis, his younger brother was proving to be a better shot than he!

Gratius visited the estate again, he liked to keep in touch with them all and to keep an eye on things, he said. He enjoyed the company of Augustus, who was also a frequent visitor and loved to hear from Gratius tales of the goings–on in the Senate in particular, and Gratius, in return, loved to hear tales of Augustus' foray into Britain, and the conquest of that heathen island on the boundaries of civilisation.

Lucia usually accompanied her husband. She had spent a lot of time on the estate during the winter helping to distribute much-needed food to the villagers, and even now was finding pockets of starvation in villages further away where the locals had not managed to survive as well as in Lydia's village, so supplies had been brought to them.

So it was all calming down, and a good harvest looked likely as the weather appeared to have returned to normal. They could now only sit and wait until harvest refilled the very depleted granary, and try and keep the birds and wild animals away from the growing crops. The rabbits were a nuisance, but the boys were able to keep the numbers down with their new archery skills, and also add some useful meat to the rather bland diet of winter.

Gratius seemed to have something on his mind, however, and when pressed admitted that he had heard talk of disquiet in the Claudius household. The emperor's mother – quite a power in the land behind the scenes – was bullying the emperor to do certain things, it was said. Gratius was not clear as to what they were, but with suspicion ripe at court, he believed there was no smoke without fire, and they should be on the lookout for trouble. Trouble came in the form of Messalina, Claudius' wife, who left her husband and married a consul called Silius. Both were discovered to be plotting against Claudius, but somebody in the entourage couldn't keep his mouth shut and the plot had been exposed. The two were duly executed, and in an attempt to hide the betrayal of his wife, Claudius blamed it on the easiest target he could find – and so expelled the very small Jewish community from Rome, banishing them on pain of death.

Gratius remarked, "What's new! We see this sort of thing again and again, getting one problem sorted out when another is just around the corner. It's usually greed and selfish behaviour that does it, as it doesn't matter to them who gets hurt. Why don't they just shut up and let us all have some peace?"

Lydia listened to him, frowning. "They never learn, do they?" she said. "Can't they see that they always lose out in the end? Did their tutors never teach them when they gave their history lessons? Or were lessons given in a way so as not to offend, avoiding the nasty bits and only telling them what was for their benefit?"

"That's about the size of it," replied Gratius, "however, I didn't come to have a moan about the aristocracy. Since the famine there have been a lot of deaths and your apartment block is now half-empty. Do you think it would be to your advantage to sell now? Or have you other plans for it?"

"I'll have to think about that one," replied Lydia. "This might be a good time to do some maintenance. I'm sure we could find tenants for it, but in the present economic situation we might have to lower the rents, as there doesn't seem to be a lot of money about at the moment. Leave it to me, perhaps now is the time to change things around a bit."

A few days later, following this conversation, Lydia found time one evening to sit on the patio for a bit of peace and quiet. She found herself thinking back to Joachim and his family, and wondered how they were getting on without the man of the house. Julia had then brought her nighttime drink, put it on the table and left Lydia to herself to enjoy the peace of the evening. As she picked up her cup of milk flavoured with honey, it was as if she heard the voice again, or was it just a thought?

Her mind continued to wander and she began to think of the followers of 'The Way' in Rome. They were such good people and would make excellent tenants for her apartment. They were so cramped where they were, and if they moved into her buildings, she could allow them the use of one of the apartments, suitably modified for them to use as a communal meeting room and place to eat. *Yes that's it*, she thought, *I'll go and see them in a few weeks and put it to them; far better to have the block used than allow it to deteriorate empty.*

She went to bed that night still thinking about it and as she dozed off the voice came again: "You make so many friends, Lydia, and that's why they love you."

Next morning she awoke thinking about her proposals for the apartment in Rome and the message from the voice: *he obviously approves,* she thought, *but this is no more than I should do for these poor people.* The rest of the day was busy, as plans for the extension of the granary had to be looked at, which she did with Marius, who turned up with the two poacher boys, who were settling in well.

Apart from one or two minor misdemeanours, the boys were proving to be good workers and she felt the time was coming when she should talk to Cassius about suitable remuneration for them. They had once or twice felt the lash of Lydia's tongue when caught out in bad behaviour, but being young and having had no moral training from a parent, she had given Marius authority to deal with them as he saw fit. They were not comfortable being reprimanded by a woman, but had the sense to realise that she was the person who could send them to the magistrates, where they would get more than a tongue lashing!

A few weeks later, Lydia turned up unexpectedly at the apartment where Joachim's widow and family lived in Rome. Lavillia opened the door to her and cried out in delight, "Oh, lady Lydia, how wonderful to see you! Is it really you? Come in."

As she came in, Lavillia started fussing around, tidying up what was already a tidy, if impoverished, apartment. Lydia laughed, "Please don't do anything for me, I've brought you a few things to help out."

Lydia then spent over an hour talking about family matters. She loved to talk about the children in particular. The conversation went on to the friends she had met the last time she visited, and of the sadness they experienced when told about the expulsion of the Jews, as two of the friends Lydia had met before were both Jews.

"But you avoided that?" observed Lydia.

"I'm not a Jew," Lavillia replied promptly, "I'm the daughter of two freed slaves, I'm a Roman," she said proudly.

She then told Lydia that they had a visitor from Judea called Silas who was a friend of Paul. "He's also a friend of Cephas," she said, "who I believe you know. If you will stay for our evening meal you will meet him. He's a lovely man and I'm sure you will like him."

Lydia agreed to come back that evening after she had had her business appointment with her agent. She gave Lavillia the supplies she had brought with her. Lavillia responded with delight, though she was almost in tears having not seen such foodstuff for over a year.

"You've had a rough time," Lydia remarked.

"Indeed we have," replied Lavillia, "but we pooled all our resources and somehow, thanks be to God, we managed to survive. A lot didn't, we had so many others to help, we often went to bed hungry."

That evening after their meal together, Silas arrived and was introduced to Lydia. Silas was a freedman, a former citizen of Damascus, and spoke both Latin and Greek. He was obviously a well-educated man, having been employed as a scribe to a branch of government for some years. He was now an assistant to a missionary teacher and was on a visit to Rome, as he put it, "to comfort the flock", and give advice and comfort to the followers living in the pagan world. The conversation was at once more intelligent than she had shared heretofore with the followers, and she felt that she must now get some answers instead of the usual bland smile and assurance that that was what the Master wanted! She intended also to question their assumption that he was the true son of God. Was that the Jewish God, or another?

Silas was a sensitive man and realised at once that Lydia's questions were not just idle curiosity, and started by asking her if she had heard of Saul, the High Priest's spymaster.

"Indeed I have," she replied, "what a dreadful man! I met him herding his helpless victims along a road to prison outside Jerusalem. He dealt with them so cruelly, with no feeling or compassion, even for the women and children he was guarding. He was like a wild animal," she said, "and I remember the lawyer Nicodemus thought little of him when I spoke to him the day before he was murdered by those thugs."

Silas smiled and said, "I think I'd better start by telling you about him first. He's called Paul now, and because of him the movement we call 'The Way' is becoming a world-wide faith."

Lydia's eyebrows shot up. "Him?" she laughed. "That dreadful man!"

Silas spent the next hour explaining the message of Paul, and how and why he had changed his stance. She slowly began to get an understanding of all she heard as the tale unfolded: the concept of sacrifice and forgiveness; the warnings and teachings against the widespread evil that seemed to pervade society; the basis of love and care for one's fellow, irrespective of who or what they were or where they came from; the concept of a full life, not slavishly adhering to old ideologies and orders given by selfish men who did not practise what they preached; living together in peace and harmony; accepting people for what they were, fellow humans, and not despising them just because they were different to you.

Lydia listened to all this open-mouthed. "But that is how I live," she said, and it seemed to her uncanny that it had to be the cause of so much dissent. "Surely that was how we should all be."

"True," said Silas, "but it took a man like the Master to get it going, because nobody had wanted to be like that before; just read the history books, my lady. Where was the golden age they all wanted? You can have it now if you want it, but the authorities won't like it. It's called the Kingdom of God!"

Lydia thought for a moment. "I do try to behave decently to all, yes it's so rewarding, but I do it for them not for me."

Silas looked at her and smiled. "You are not far from that kingdom," he said. "It's within all of us, but we have to seek it out, before we find it!"

It was getting late; the sun had set and Lydia's guard and transport would be wanting to get on the road. Just before she left, she remembered her plan for her apartments and told them it would go ahead in a few weeks and she would let them know as soon as it was all finalised. Those present were ecstatic with joy, while Silas praised the idea, saying, "Let us all give thanks to God for his mercies and for sending lady Lydia to us in our time of need."

Lydia eventually arrived home at midnight, having had what she felt was a most worthwhile day. As she slept that night, the voice came to her again, saying, "Lydia, well done."

She awoke later, with the sudden thought that the followers of 'The Way' were making it all too complicated. *Surely the message is simplicity itself: love your God and your fellow humans as yourself. Yet they are all beginning to talk about ceremonies like initiation rites, by being immersed in water, and eating ceremonial bread. The Jews do all that, and it's only those things that matter to the Jews, and not how they treat each other. When we were in Judea, they wouldn't talk to us unless they had to, and openly said they despised us. The message seems to be, "This is what you must do or you can't join us", and that's not what the Master wanted, surely. Why are they making it complicated? Why are they making theology of it. The Master wasn't a theologian so far as I can tell; he just loved his fellow men and wanted all to emulate him. He didn't say, "This is what you must do", he said, "This is what you should do if you love God and your fellow men. Use your God–given brain! If you love God you'll do all these right things as a natural part of life!" Part of the follower's aim, it seemed to her, was certainly to do good, but so as to earn a reward; Heaven, they called it. Why can't they understand that the message is not how to die, but how to live!*

But if Saul is now Paul, that could only have been caused by divine influence – knowing what an evil man he appeared to be! His whole life is now changed, and as a very clever Jewish theologian himself, that is a marvel! Was it from him that Silas had to learn all he knows?

It was winter again. The year was now almost over and had given them another bumper harvest, so that the modified granary was full to overflowing. There was even plenty of wine, and looking back to that dreadfully wet summer, Marius was surprised that the vines had not been stricken with mildew and killed off, but they had survived and there was now a plentiful supply of wine for domestic consumption, with plenty to go on sale to fulfil all the contracts.

Both of Augustus' boys were growing up quickly. They had not spent quite so much time in the boat this year as their studies increased, and their father had insisted that they gave more time to their school work. Meanwhile Lucia, now that she wasn't needed to supervise them, spent more time at the villa with Lydia.

Lucia was interested in Lydia's plans for the apartment in the capital and offered to help Lydia in any way she could. As Lydia told her, things didn't just happen overnight and a lot of thought had to go into the project before she contacted her agents to arrange the re – letting and modification of one apartment for a meeting room. Lydia knew she had to reassure them of the credibility of the new tenants, and that although they were not rich people, they were scrupulously honest and would pay their rents on time. But as she said, she was unable to see the arrangements being actioned for the time being, and it would probably not happen before the end of spring at the earliest.

Marius and his fellow workers and their families

were all invited by Lydia to the usual midwinter festival party at the villa. These were never noisy affairs, but the wives loved them as they could get together and chat about family matters, and Lydia enjoyed their company. The women were always aware that Lydia was their husbands' employer, though rarely overstepped the mark so far as familiarity was concerned. When the occasional slips happened Lydia took it in good part and usually put it down to nerves due to being in such rich surroundings – she knew how much they appreciated her concern for their welfare.

So the new year started well, but unforeseen troubles arose and a severe measles outbreak among the workers' children caused much distress. Many of the children were affected and it took weeks to subside. By the time it ended they had lost two little ones, two became profoundly deaf, one was paralysed, and some developed a severe skin rash that would not clear with the medicines available. However, Lydia and Lucia worked hard, visiting the affected families, bringing treats to the children and a welcome shoulder to cry on for the mothers. The planting had to go ahead irrespective of family ill health and was completed by the end of spring with the weather looking set to produce another good harvest.

Lydia's plan for the apartments had gone ahead after consultation with her agents. The apartments were now occupied, with over half of the tenants followers of 'The Way.' There had been no problems, but there was trouble at court: Emperor Claudius, being fed up living on his own without a companion since he killed his wife, had decided to marry again. He had married his niece

Agripinna, who already had a son called Domitus, and there was now some strife in the family between Domitus and Claudius' two children by Messalina. Domitus , Agripinnas' son, was the only surviving direct descendant of the famous Emperor Augustus, and palace watchers were already predicting trouble when it came to succession. Apparently Agripinna was a nasty piece of work and was felt to be capable of some form of skulduggery in the future.

However, the work on the apartments now being finished, a celebration of the event was arranged to take place on Midsummer's day, and Lydia invited Gratius, Lucia and Marius to join her to see her latest project. Gratius did not know a lot about Lydia's plan for the apartments, but when she explained it to him in detail, he was not overly impressed.

"You are setting apart an identifiable group in the middle of the city," he began. "These people would be far better left mixed in with the general population, because in the event of trouble, their exclusivity will be perceived by the locals as a cause for concern. This will precipitate their downfall; it's happened before. It's a nice idea, but with the Emperor playing God, and this lot saying they worship another God, there's going to be competition, and when things do go wrong, they'll be a soft target for jealous and greedy men."

The party came and went. Gratius did attend out of curiosity, but he came in casual clothing so that nobody was aware of his position or rank. Lydia was pleased that he had attended and seen the result of her philanthropy. Remarkably, he said he found the whole thing quite refreshing, observing afterwards that there had been no nastiness, backbiting or even friction. "These people seem to have got something" was his prognosis.

Marius, however, had no trouble enjoying himself. As an ex-army man used to a disciplined life, he thought these people were marvellously disciplined. There were no ugly incidents like at other events he had attended, and Lucia too thought the whole thing to be wonderful!

Over the next few years, the apartment project and the estate flourished. Time passed pleasantly for all with good harvests, good weather, and an increase in the number of followers of 'The Way'. As Lydia got older she felt she had made a satisfactory contribution to the happiness and harmony of her society.

One day the news broke that Emperor Claudius had been assassinated – by his present wife, it was reported. In a palace coup, her son Domitus had been appointed Emperor, and had taken the name Nero.

CHAPTER 15

Life for the followers of 'The Way', now called Christians after the Christos, was good. There was little if any interference from the authorities, and so long as they kept their heads down for a few years, they would prosper.

Meanwhile the new Emperor, with the help of two senior advisers, who were both philosophers, managed the affairs of the state well, even though his mother, Agripinna, had persisted in trying to interfere in state matters. Her interference was always usually countered by his two trusted wise men, but one day Nero had a flaming row with her and she went too far, so he locked her in a room until she backed down. After a week she still had not, so he had her executed.

The thought of opposition rarely bothered him, and to make sure there was no problem, Claudius' son Britanicus was also executed. He now expected all his troubles to be over, but unfortunately both his advisers left the scene; one died and Seneca, his most influential counsellor, retired from the political scene due to ill health. These two men had guided the ship of state through calm waters, but without them, stormy seas lay ahead and Nero now went his own way.

Eventually disaster struck, but not before he had the mad idea of having a public holiday to boost his popularity. This was designed by him to give the masses some fun, with spectacular parades, special religious ceremonies and displays in the arena with himself playing a major role. He had one massive procession consisting of a mobile altar on a cart pulled by six white donkeys, on which burnt sacrifices were given to numerous gods as it went along.

Unfortunately this hit an obstruction in the uneven road, right in the middle of a densely populated part of the city, and it turned over, spilling the burning coals and oil onto the road. This promptly set fire to the wooden houses on either side of the road. The fire spread and eventually engulfed a quarter of the city, burning it to the ground. This did not, of course, enhance his popularity as so many of the plebs, for whose benefit this day was supposed to be, felt aggrieved at the loss of not only their homes, but a lot of businesses and their employment.

However, Lydia's block, being a stone-built edifice – her husband had known what he was doing when he purchased it – was untouched by the fire, and apart from smoke damage was unharmed. Neither were any of her tenants injured, although hundreds of other citizens were killed or injured by falling timbers.

The fact that the block where the Christians lived was not destroyed created the suspicion among the general population that it was either under some form of divine protection, or that some sort of sorcery had been used to cause the fire. Perhaps it was the result of treasonous behaviour because they denied the divinity of the emperor, or because they were a secret society who never mixed with anybody other than their own group and therefore were most likely to be the cause of the fire!

Hearing the sounds of discontent among the plebs, Nero bestirred himself, and with an advisor went to have a look at the devastation. He had received a blow to his pride now that events had ended like this; this was not what he had intended, and when he saw Lydia's block unscathed he demanded to know whose it was and why it had not been damaged. His advisor told him it was owned by a patrician lady called Lydia, but was occupied by a new group called Christians who worshipped a god that was unknown to Rome.

Nero turned to the man and asked him what he thought should be done. The advisor, who had most of his money in rented property, the majority of which had burned to the ground, saw his opportunity to get hold of this stone building and advised Nero to put the blame of the fire on these people, saying, "After all, they wouldn't burn their own place down, would they?"

Nero thought about it and said, "Right, I'll get that lot and blame them for it!"

On a visit to see Lydia, Gratius told her about the fire and warned her to beware. As he had told her before, her tenants were an identifiable group and likely to get some blame. He advised her to get her tenants out to a place of safety away from Rome before anything nasty happened.

Lydia was most distressed. "I must go and see for myself," she said firmly, "and see what I can do to help."

Gratius replied hurriedly, "No, you must not, Lydia, use your common sense. The Emperor is going to look for scapegoats, so just send a message to your people to get out now."

But Lydia was unsure if her agents would be able to find alternative accommodation for so many in the circumstances, but she hoped she might use her influence to help these poor people with her few remaining connections at court. No, she must go herself!

So Lydia went, and saw the surrounding damage with her block unharmed in the middle of it all. She was met by the leader of the group and was told of abuse and stone-throwing at the followers, and that one young lad had been set upon by a mob who accused them all of witchcraft. The boy had been badly injured.

As such, Lydia asked for them all to come to the meeting hall that evening to discuss the future. The meeting started with a prayer of thanks for their survival, but the one hundred or so worried people all had something to say – some trusted in God to help, but others felt it was right to stay and testify to their faith. In the end Lydia clapped her hands for silence and told them that common sense said that they should all come with her to her estate until it blew over.

Suddenly the door to the room was kicked open and a group of soldiers under the command of a centurion burst in. "By command of the emperor you are all under arrest for arson," he shouted. "Get out into the courtyard all of you, move, move, move!"

"Not you," he said rudely to Lydia, "the emperor wants to see you." She got up to move. "Sit down!" he shouted.

"Don't you dare talk to me like that," she returned furiously.

"I'll talk to you anyway I like, as I do to all criminals. Shut up, or I will make you shut up." he shouted at her. The centurion searched the room but could find nothing that interested him, so he grunted and said, "Get outside, you're going to the palace so keep quiet."

"Where are my friends?" she said, ignoring his words.

"On the way to prison, where they and people like you belong. Now out," he snarled.

She was marched across the gutted landscape to the palace, taken into the main guardroom, and pushed unceremoniously into a cell which contained only a wooden bed and a bucket. Lydia heard the door slammed and locked behind her. She collapsed onto the wooden bench and burst into tears. Tired, hungry and humiliated, she sat on the bed in despair .

Suddenly she heard the voice: "I will tell you what to say, the words will be put into your mouth. We will meet soon, and then all will be well." They were strangely comforting, those words, and she went to sleep with that reassurance.

It was the morning of the Emperor's audience at the palace when chosen citizens were allowed to petition the Emperor. Those who were chosen and ushered into the regal presence were few and far between, chosen with great care to make a petition that would, if granted, enhance the reputation of the emperor. But occasionally someone who had made an impact, for good or ill, was also brought before him for the purpose of examining his views or ideas.

This day it was the turn of a senior army officer who had just returned from active service on the island of Britain. He was told to recount his part in the humiliation of Queen Boudicca and her daughters when captured by the army, after the revolt they had lead against the occupying legions. Nero wanted to know in intimate and disgusting detail what horror had been perpetrated upon these women, and when told in graphic detail what had happened, he laughed and cheered as each appalling act was revealed.

The official presiding over the ceremony was then asked if there was anyone else to come before the emperor, and was told there was the wife of the late Pontius Pilate. She had, said the man, supported belief in a strange god unknown to Rome, and was also accused of arson, in that she and her followers had started the fire that had devastated a quarter of Rome's housing.

"Show her in," demanded Nero, expecting another display of unpleasantness to titillate his jaded palate.

Lydia was dragged out of her cell and paraded before her emperor. He was surprised to see such a small, grey-haired, elderly women before him. "And what have you been up to?" he asked unpleasantly, "You and your followers are the ones who burnt half of my city to the ground, are you not?"

By now, Lydia was tired, thoroughly fed up, hungry and scruffy. She looked this chubby-faced teenage-looking man up and down, but could see no mercy in his eyes, so refused to answer.

This attitude unsettled Nero, who was used to people grovelling before him. "Speak up, woman, your emperor demands it!" he roared.

Lydia thought for a moment. "They are not my followers," she retorted bravely. "They follow the Christos, who wants nothing more than peace and harmony for all men."

"Really?" sneered Nero. "Peace and harmony? That's a good one. So how do we get that, by burning down Rome?"

"We did not, and you know we did not, God doesn't

want war; he wants all men to live in peace with each other!" she replied firmly.

"Oh and which god is this then?" he laughed. "I'm a god and will do what I want, not what you want. Take her away, guard, and bring her to my box at the circus this afternoon."

Lydia was returned roughly to her cell, a crust of bread and a handful of grapes thrown in at her. She sat trembling on the bed and thought, *I don't know how I said that to that man, but the voice said I'd be given the words and I suppose those were them.*

That afternoon, she was taken to the arena and pushed into the emperor's box.

"Right, here you are. Now stay with me and watch the fun," he smirked.

He clapped his hands, and two men ran across the sandy space below. They opened a door and beckoned the occupants out onto the sand; a group of people – men, women and children – came out and were herded into a circle and made to sit down. Lydia gasped in dismayed surprise, as she recognized these people to be some of her tenants. However, the huge audience who sat in tiered rows around her were expecting gladiators and started a slow handclapping; they didn't want to see a lot of old men, women and children, they wanted blood!

Nero turned to Lydia. "So am I a god or not?" he asked sneering. "Because if I am, I can do what I want. If not, let's see what your god can do!"

Lydia, dreading what was about to happen, said shakily, "No you are not a god, but I know who is. He is the father of the Christos and creator of all."

Nero smiled again, "Well, let's see if he can save that lot," he gestured to her friends below, "because if he is so powerful, we are now going to find out."

With that, he disdainfully clapped his hands again and another door into the arena opened. Three fully grown African lions, which had been starved for three days, leapt out, attacked the group savagely and within five minutes had torn them all to pieces to the delight of the cheering audience.

Lydia felt faint, but she pulled herself together, aghast at what she had seen. Nero laughed at her distress. "Well, your god didn't help them, did he?"

Lydia felt something come over her. "You wicked, evil man," she said, tears running down her face. "May God forgive you. When you meet Him you will cringe for mercy. May he give it to you, though you will not deserve it. Yes, one day you will die and then will have to answer in front of Him for your wickedness."

Nero rose out of his chair in fury, his face red, angry and eyes bulging,

"Take her away!" he shrieked. "Take her out and cut her throat."

Lydia was dragged out of the box, a guard pulled back her head by her hair and she heard the swish of a sword. The world exploded in a cascade of coloured lights, and then slowly faded as she dropped down, and down, into merciful oblivion.

CHAPTER 16

It was pleasant sitting beside the sea. A few small waves broke gently on the white sand of the beach, and a gentle breeze blew from the land rustling the palm fronds behind her, which sheltered her from the sun. Birds were singing, and she felt at peace.

She did not recognise where she was, it was new to her, but looking out across the water to the other side of what was obviously a bay, she could make out what appeared to be a city or large town. Its walls were shining white and its spires and domes of gold reflected the sunlight. As she listened she heard the sound of melodious singing to the accompaniment of harps coming from the city.

There was a large sailing boat tacking back and forth across the water. It had a red and white hull with light blue-coloured sails, and she could just make out the crew raising and lowering the sails as necessary. As it got nearer she was able to see two figures in the bows standing side by side, a man and a woman dressed in what appeared to be golden apparel.

She watched as it slowly came closer, eventually moving into shallow water and grounding a small distance from where she sat. As it came to rest, the two people stepped out of the boat into the shallow water and waded ashore.

Lydia stood up and walked down the beach toward

them. Suddenly she gasped in recognition; these two beautiful, young people were her mother and father as she remembered them from her childhood and they threw themselves into each other's arms.

"Mother! Father!" she gasped as they hugged each other closely.

"Oh, well done, Lydia," said her father, "we are now all together again."

Her mother smiled that gentle smile she so well remembered. "Lydia, my one and only darling daughter, how lovely you look," she said gently.

"Where are we going?" she asked as they climbed on board the boat. The sails were hoisted and they sped across the water toward the city.

"Home," replied her father, smiling broadly. "You just wait and see."

The boat edged up to the quayside, where the singing was louder, and she could see the singers standing on the city walls. They stepped off the boat onto a quayside covered with beautifully manicured lawns and flower beds full of brilliant blooms. With her mother and father hand-in-hand, they all walked towards the city gates, which were massive golden gates with a small postern in the centre of one of them. As they reached the gates the postern opened and out came two young people. Both were wearing the same gold cloaks that her parents wore, and they escorted them up to the gates.

One called out, "Open the gates, my Lord," and as the gates slowly rolled back, there stood a tall man dressed all in white with a crown on his head. He had black hair, bright blue eyes, and a small mole on his chin.

Lydia stared at him in disbelief. "It's him," she

breathed. It was the man in her dream of all those years ago, and as soon as he spoke, she knew it was truly him.

With a smile he said, "Welcome to my father's home Lydia, and welcome to the reward that you have earned." He smiled again and gestured to the two young people, who came forward and put a golden cloak around her shoulders and a crown on her head. "You must be appropriately attired to meet my father," he said.

"What have I done to deserve this?" she gasped.

He replied gently, "You gave your life for many, I gave my life for you all."

Suddenly the trumpets sounded, the singing rose to a crescendo, and with her mother and father, Lydia followed her Lord into the city. There they were met by a huge crowd all dressed in gold and wearing crowns. Some she recognised: there was Joachim, there was Nicodemus with a broad smile on his face looking thirty years younger, oh, and there was Miriam of her Jerusalem days, there were her friends from the apartments, and the two little boys lost with measles... all together, safe and sound, in their Master's kingdom.